Jake and Sam
At The Empty Abbey

Jinny Powers Berten

Illustrated by Elizabeth W. Schott

Fountain Square
Publishing LLC: Cincinnati

Text copyright ©2006 by Jinny Powers Berten

Illustrations copyright ©2006 by Elizabeth W. Schott

All rights reserved. Published by Fountain Square Publishing LLC: Cincinnati

Manufactured in the United States of America
Library of Congress Control Number: 2006906688
ISBN 9780972442114

Illustrations: Elizabeth W. Schott   www.ewschott-fineart.com
Cover design: Elizabeth W. Schott, Page design: ElizabethW. Schott

Printed in the U.S.A.
Second American Edition, 2010

Fountain Square Publishing LLC: Cincinnati

fspcincinnati@aol.com
www.fountainsquarepublishing.com

For the special ones:
John, Samantha, Isabelle, Andrew
and Poppie too.

My thanks to many people who helped this book
become a reality: Susie Heinz, Kaki Donahue,
Jen Donahue, Grace Ward, Janet Turner,
Maureen Conlan, Kathy Bunnell and Sandy Cohan,
for the generous gift of their time and thoughts; my
readers, Jake, Sam, Isabelle, Ellen and the students
at Benjamin Franklin and Prince of Peace Schools,
who provided me with their children's perspective;
Joan Seller, for her British critique; my ever patient
and always creative illustrator, Beth Schott and
my husband, John, whose encouragement and
insight helped bring this book to life.

Also by Jinny Powers Berten

Littsie of Cincinnati
Littsie and the Underground Railroad

Goodnight Children Everywhere

Goodnight children, everywhere
Your Mummy thinks of you tonight
Though you are far away
She's with you night and day.
Goodnight children everywhere.

Goodnight children everywhere
Your Daddy thinks of you tonight.
And though you are far away
You'll go home one day.
Goodnight children, everywhere.

song written by Rogers and Phillips
published by J. Norris

Jake and Sam
At The Empty Abbey

Chapter 1

THE COTTAGE
AT PEVENSEY

Softly the snow fell, piling in corners of windows, covering the roof of the garden shed, and making pyramids on the square posts of the fence that surrounded the cottage. The wind swept through the cracks in the cottage and chilled the air around the sleeping boy who lay on a mattress on the floor. Jake rolled over under the thin blanket and whispered, "Sam, are you awake?"

His sister didn't answer. "She probably needs a bit more sleep," thought Jake. "Wearing those leg braces is tiring; something Miss Bottomley doesn't seem to understand."

At age eight, Jake's sister was two years younger than Jake. Everyone called her Sam even though her real name was Samantha Marie. She had contracted polio when she was a baby, leaving her legs weak and a bit crooked. The heavy iron braces she wore helped her walk.

Jake listened to the soft sounds of Sam's breath mingling with the sound of the wind as it whined around the corners of the old cottage. He thought about home. He missed it so. He missed his Mum's good cooking, his Dad's jokes, the fireplace, his books, the children's playground in Kensington Gardens, fairy cakes, lollies his Nanna bought for him; but most of all he missed his dog, Whidbey. Though Whidbey could hardly be considered beautiful, he was quite smart and he fancied being with Jake, especially when they ran together in the open spaces around Speaker's Corner in Hyde Park.

"I wish Hitler would turn into a sausage that I could feed to Whidbey," thought Jake. It was January, 1940, a very bad man named, Adolph Hitler, ruled Germany and he wanted to rule the whole world. He and his army had already taken the countries of Austria and Czechoslovakia. In September he had invaded Poland; it was then that England went to war. Hitler had bombed Poland horribly and he was probably going to bomb England too, especially London. The government and the King had made a plan so that children could get out of London and be safe. They were to be sent to the country where they would live with people who had offered to give them a home. After thinking about it for a very long time, Jake's Mum and Dad signed their children on. They felt it was best. And even though the children would be living with strangers and would be terribly missed, they would at least be safe, out of harm's way and out of the reach of Hitler's terrible bombs. And that is how Jake and Sam came to live in Miss Bottomley's house on the edge of the village of Pevensey.

Jake remembered the day they left London. His Mum had dressed him and Sam in their warmest clothes and filled a nice suitcase with other things they would need: underwear, toothbrushes, blankets, Jake's teddy, Sam's doll Emma, and a picture of Mum, Dad and Whidbey in front of their house in Notting Hill. They each had a bag of sandwiches and fruit. And, they also carried gas masks in a cardboard box over their shoulder, just in case Hitler should decide to drop his terrible gas bombs. "I'll bet Hitler lets go terrible gas himself, the worst that any human being has ever made. I feel sorry for his wife," thought Jake. Jake remembered how Mum and Dad had walked them to the train station, all the while acting as though they were going on a great adventure. But Jake could see tears in his Mum's eyes and he noticed that his Dad kept a straight face. When the family had arrived at the station, a large crowd of children had already gathered on the platform. Each child had a suitcase and a label attached to his coat with his name and address on it. Jake was very quiet that morning but silly Sam just kept chattering away as if they were going on holiday. Jake was old enough to know that this was no holiday. He remembered all the children piling onto the train, he remembered a few teachers going along to help them get settled in their new homes. He remembered looking out the window as the train pulled away and seeing all the parents waving and watching his Dad hold his Mum tight.

And then that awful part when they got to Pevensey. After their train had pulled into the station and the children had piled off, their teacher led them into the station house. There were about twenty

children in all. Jake remembered the day as a bright and sunny one, a beautiful day. The building was filled with light, making everything seem hopeful. At one end of the room stood a group of adults all talking and looking a bit curious. The teacher told the children to stand at the opposite end of the room, to stand straight and tall and try to look their best. The children, unsure of what lay ahead, suddenly grew quiet. The teacher announced that the adults should come forward and choose which child they wanted. Several of the adults came forward straight away and made a choice. One woman stood in front of Jake and Sam and said she would take the boy but not the girl. Jake held Sam's hand tightly and in his strongest voice said, "No, we stay together. My Mum and Dad said we must stay together." The lady walked on to the next child. Jake and Sam watched as each of the other children was chosen and as groups of children and adults left the building and headed into the bright sunshine. They stood alone at the end of the room. For the rest of his life Jake would not forget how awful it was standing there. He was embarrassed that no one had chosen them, he was angry that people had not taken them because of Sam's leg braces, he was sad into the very insides of his body, so sad that he couldn't even cry.

Suddenly a woman bounded through the doors and screeched, "Am I too late for the little vaccies?" She was a big woman, looked somewhat like a chicken, with enormous breasts, skinny little legs, a beak for a nose and feathery red hair. She wore a dirty purple dress with yellow polka dots. Her stockings were rolled down to her ankles. In her hand she carried a leather bag and inside was a ferret.

Jake's teacher came forward and said, "Excuse me, the children are not 'vaccies.' They are called evacuees because they had to be evacuated from London. Thank you very much. Jake and Sam are the only children left."

I knew I should have gotten here earlier," said Miss Alvira Bottomley. "I guess they will have to do. I get the end of the litter, plus one with braces," she said as she looked more closely at Sam. "Now what am I going to do with this blonde?" she asked, pointing a dirty finger at Sam.

"She stays with me," said Jake, looking Miss Bottomley right in her beady eyes.

"A bit brash, aren't you, boy?" whispered Miss

Bottomley so that the teacher could not hear. "If she comes, you will have to do the work that she can't do."

And then with a pudding sweet voice, Miss Bottomley announced to the teacher, "These two are darling, such sweet faces. Yes, I will be glad to take them. Come along, children."

As Jake's teacher gave Miss Bottomley some papers, he pleaded with his eyes not to make them go. But the teacher did not look at him and out the door he and Sam went, pulled along by the nasty woman.

Miss Bottomley dragged the children through the village, past the post office, the sweet shop, the butcher, and the church, up a small hill and over a stone bridge to a thatched cottage that sat alongside the railroad tracks. It was a tired old house that had not been tended to for a very long time. The garden was overgrown, the yellow paint on the cottage was peeling off in big patches, several windows were broken, and the front door was so wonky it could not be closed. There was no electricity in the house; the nearest bathroom was in a shed outside. The first floor had two rooms, a big kitchen and a bedroom for Miss Bottomley. Upstairs was the loft where Jake lay, thinking about home.

His thoughts were interrupted by noises coming from downstairs. "Oh, stuff and bother," thought Jake, "she is up and she will want me to put the kettle on for her tea, toast her some bread and boil her an egg. Mum would be surprised how well I can cook. Then The Bottom will want Sam to make her bed and if it isn't done fast enough, we won't get any breakfast."

He turned quickly and shook Sam. "Wake up, wake up, Sam. She is up and about. Quick, I'll help you put on your braces."

Sam yawned and moved slowly from under the covers. "It is snowing Jake...snow. Maybe she'll let us play in it."

"And when has she ever let us play before?"

"Get out of your beds you lazy brats," yelled Miss Bottomley from the bottom of the stairs. The children knew that she would never come up because she hated climbing stairs, her knees hurt her, and she was too lazy. "There's work to do," she went on, "and if I don't hear your feet on the floor in five seconds, I'll send up my sweetie pie to get you up."

"Jake, don't let her send up Fulham," pleaded Sam. "Please, please, it scares me so."

"Don't be frightened," Jake soothed his sister. "That is just what she wants. I pretend to be frightened so she thinks Fulham is scaring me. Actually I have grown to like the ferret and he likes me. But we won't let The Bottom know that. Watch this."

"No, no, Miss Bottomley, please don't let the ferret loose," Jake whimpered. "Please, please don't," he called, as if he were crying.

With that, Miss Bottomley flung open the door and screamed, "Go get 'em, Fulham."

There was a great thrashing and the sound of animal toenails could be heard on the steps as the ferret raced up the stairs.

"No, no," screamed Jake as he held his arms out to the ferret and smiled at Sam. Fulham snuggled right underneath Jake's blanket.

"Please, Miss Bottomley," pleaded Sam.

"That will teach you to get up straight away the next time," said Miss Bottomley, slamming the door to the loft.

Jake played hide and seek with the ferret under the blanket. Then he held him gently and stroked his beautiful soft, full coat. Fulham was a red-eyed, white ferret. He enjoyed hopping, jumping and playing with Jake. The soft clucking sounds he made signified the ferret's happiness at being with the children.

"Quick," Jake said to Sam, "let's get your braces on. She will be yelling again any minute."

He put the ferret down gently and helped Sam as she tried to get her stiff legs into the heavy braces. They were difficult to put on and once they were on, Jake had to help her stand up. That wasn't easy. The ferret hopped on his shoulder as he worked and nibbled on his ear. The Bottom, as he called Miss Bottomley, didn't know he had trained Fulham to do that, nor did she know that sometimes Fulham got into Jake's pocket.

"See," Jake said to Sam. "He really is nice. There is nothing to be afraid of."

"But he smells so awful," said Sam. "Nasty!"

"Only sometimes," said Jake. "Here, touch him."

With some hesitation, Sam stroked the animal. "I do like his short little legs," she said. "They are cute."

"You'll grow to like all of him some day," said Jake, shivering as he pulled on his clothes. He was so glad that his mother had sent a lovely woolly sweater with him. Even though it was getting a bit small for him now, it kept him warm on those cool days when the wind blew in strongly from the sea. He was glad he had it, for he was certain that The Bottom would never buy him one.

"I'm ready," said Sam walking unsteadily toward the door. "Stay with me, Jake. You know how she is."

"I'm right here," said Jake as they went down the stairs and into the warm kitchen, with Fulham running behind them. Actually, it could have been a very nice kitchen with a big fireplace, a lovely dresser filled with china, a big black cooker and an ample sized table in the middle of the room. It would have been warm and inviting if Miss Bottomley had made the slightest effort to tidy it up. Instead it was filled with old newspapers, the occasional butter wrapper, dead flowers, piles of egg shells, candle stubs, apple cores, chicken bones and dried porridge and tons of other disgusting and nasty things. Off to one side on the kitchen counter was Fulham's cage.

This morning Miss Bottomley sat sprawled in a chair by the fireplace reading her newspaper, still dressed in her purple night-gown and cap. She really did like purple.

"Get this fire started," she snarled at Jake. "What's

taking you so long? I am cold and I don't like to be cold. You know that, don't you, Jake?" she asked.

"Yes, Miss Bottomley," Jake said, quickly pulling twigs and logs from the pile and stacking them in the fireplace.

"And what are you standing there for, Missy? Get in there and make my bed and I don't want to see one wrinkle anywhere. No help from your brother either. I want him to do other things."

As Jake lit the fire, the logs roared into comforting flames, but it turned suddenly and the whole cottage began to fill with smoke. He'd forgotten to open the chimney flue and the smoke had blown right back down into the room.

While Miss Bottomley began to cough and sputter, Sam calmly walked to the front door and opened it.

"You dumb lout!" Miss Bottomley screamed at Jake. "Open the flue. Open it now I say!"

"But Miss Bottomley," Jake began, his eyes starting to water from the smoke, "I can't. Its too hot!"

"Open it," she commanded, taking his hand and thrusting it toward the vent. "Open it or you will feel the end of this poker," she said, as she picked up the fire tool and put it in the flames.

Bending low she gave him a good kick on his bottom, and he fell forward and grabbed the handle of the vent. The scorching heat of the hot metal made him pull back quickly. But not soon enough. The pain shot through his body and centered on his hand. He had been burned badly. His hand was red; he couldn't straighten it out. Tears welled in his eyes but he was determined not to let Miss Bottomley see him cry. Jake held his hand tightly and lifted his head and looked right at her without saying a word.

It was Miss Bottomley who broke the silence. "I don't know why I ever said you could come here. You aren't worth anything and your sister even less. I was so kind to take you and then you act like this. You should be back in London with Hitler's bombs. I've a mind to send you tomorrow. Go, get out of here, the both of you. And don't you come back till dark. I don't care if school is out earlier. I can't stand to look at you. You don't appreciate anything." And with that, she pushed them out the front door. "Here," she yelled after them. "I'm sending Fulham with you. He'll keep you in line. Bite their toes once in while, give them a good scare, Fulham," she laughed.

Chapter 2

A FRIEND FOUND

The children fell out into the snow; no coats or hats or warm mittens or long mufflers. This was not the first time that this had happened to them, and they knew that if they hurried to school, at least they might find some warmth there. So they struggled to run. As they turned the corner, out of sight of Miss Bottomley's house, Jake leaned against a wall and examined his hand. Beginning to blister, it looked quite ugly. He could not move it at all. Fulham was walking around his feet as if to ask what was going on. Jake stooped to pick him up and as he did so, Fulham seemed to notice the burnt hand and began to lick it.

"Oh, Jake look... he feels so sorry for you."

"Actually the licking does make my hand feel a bit better," said Jake. "But I don't know if he can help all that much. It feels pretty awful." He stroked the ferret with his good hand and then put him in his pocket for the walk to school. He bent and picked up snow; it cooled his burnt skin a bit.

The brother and sister walked along the old city wall and up the hill. As they started to cross the bridge, a hail of snowballs fell on them. Three of the schools bullies had been waiting for them under the bridge.

"Vaccies, vaccies," they taunted.

Jake returned as many missiles as he could, considering he had a burnt hand. Sam was unsteady on her feet and could not get to the snow quickly enough. Fulham began hissing out of fear and crouched lower in Jake's pocket. The children were used to this name calling; some of the village children did not like vaccies coming into their school, making them sit two to a seat, taking more of the teachers' attention and generally disrupting their normal schedule. By now, however, most of the children had come around and understood that if they had lived in

London they too might have had to leave, and besides, they didn't like Hitler either. They were glad to help out children just like themselves. Unfortunately, there were still a few who liked to torment the newcomers and here they were today back to their old tricks. And they had picked the worst of all days, what with Jake's burnt hand, no coats or hats, no breakfast, none of the makings for lunch, and a hissing ferret in Jake's pocket. The snowballs were flying all around them, soosh, splat and crunch. Sam slipped in the snow, her braced legs flying out from under her. Dogs from the surrounding houses and cottages began to bark and disturb the quiet village.

Just as Jake thought that the boys were surely going to come and push their faces right down into the deepest part of the cold snow, he looked up to see the familiar brown skirts of a monk flying toward them. The old man quickly scooped up snow and flung missiles at the bullies. Their hats were knocked off straight away. Snow hit them in the most damaging strategic spots.

"Go on now," he yelled in the gravelly voice that the children had all learned to fear. "Surely you don't

want your parents to know about this, but they will, if I see you doing it again. You can bet on that, laddies," he called as the boys ran out of sight.

The monk stood the two children up and pushed them toward the schoolhouse, mumbling all the way about snow, children, parents, early morning and his need of a cup of tea. "Well now," he said to the children as he opened the school door, "you have to learn to keep away from the likes of them. They are up to no good. I am afraid they will torment people for the rest of their lives. Now here, sit down and I will start the fire. Have to do it anyway. Do it every morning so the school will be warm when you get here," he said, as he shoveled coal into the stove that would warm the classroom for the day.

As the fire caught hold and began to give off heat, the children huddled closer to the stove and at last relaxed a bit in its warmth. Jake could feel Fulham relax too as he stretched in his pocket. They were not really afraid of the monk that everyone called Godric for they had often seen his eyes sparkle in merriment. And hadn't he saved them today?

The monk had a workshop that was attached to the school building on one side and next to the remains of the old abbey on the other. He had many odd jobs: taking care of the school building, looking after a community garden and, his favorite occupation, tending to the remains of the old abbey. He came now out of his workshop with a steaming cup of tea and a piece of hot toast dripping with honey. Taking a seat on one of the small benches, he said to Jake and Sam, "I need to know more about you. I take it you are not from around here."

"No, Brother Godric," said Jake. "We're vaccies from London."

"London," said Brother Godric, "it is a good town but I suppose not so good now that Hitler is up to his tricks. The wireless has been talking day and night about his antics. Who has taken you in here?"

"The Bottom! I mean Miss Bottomley," said Jake quickly.

"My feelings exactly," mumbled Brother Godric, as he took a bite from the toast. "She must feed you all right, she feeds herself well enough."

Jake and Sam made no reply but felt their stomachs rumble as the monk took yet another bite.

"So Jake," Godric said, licking honey from his lips. "What have you got in your pocket? Is that lunch?"

"No sir, it's a ferret. Miss Bottomley's ferret."

"A ferret? I thought I smelled something!" the monk roared. "You might know Miss Bottomley would have a ferret."

"That's how I feel," said Sam. "It's disgusting."

"No it isn't," said Jake. "Remember how it helped my hand this morning, Sam?", Jake said in Fulham's defense?

"What happened to your hand?" asked Godric

"Oh nothing, really," said Jake. He didn't want Godric talking to The Bottom because then they would really get punished.

"Might I see the nasty ferret?" asked Godric.

"Of course," said Jake and reached in his pocket to retrieve Fulham. "See, isn't he beautiful?" he asked, as he handed Godric the sleek, white, red-eyed animal that did indeed carry a distinct smell.

"Yes, he is handsome, but I also see that your hand has been burnt and quite badly. How did that happen?"

Jake told the monk part of the story but didn't let on how really horrible Miss Bottomley had been that morning.

"And," said the monk, "did you get any breakfast

this morning?"

"No sir," said Sam quickly as the monk ate his last bite of toast.

"And did you bring lunch?"

"No sir," said Sam "Miss Bottomley usually doesn't give us lunch except when she is in a good mood and then we might have a boiled potato and cabbage."

Jake gave Sam a look that told her she had said too much and he quickly tried to change the subject. "Look, Brother Godric, the snow has stopped."

"Now wait just a minute," said Brother Godric. "I don't want to talk about the snow. I want to talk about The Bottom. She doesn't give you breakfast or lunch. And what about dinner?"

Sam was only too happy to keep on talking . "Oh, we do eat dinner, usually porridge and bread and a little milk. But you know if we are bad we have to stand and watch her eat her dinner. She always has, every night, lovely roast and potatoes, yummy veggies and oh the absolute best puddings. Puddings like our Mum used to make, but all we get is the smell of them while we watch her eat."

The monk's face clouded over. He thumped one of the desks so hard that you could hear the wood cracking. "What a beast of a woman! Taking advantage of young children who had to escape from Hitler's bombs. Probably working you to death. I am going to see about this," he said as he started looking for his coat.

"No, sir, please," cried Jake, running to stop him. "It won't work. Our teacher tried to talk to her once, and we paid dearly for it. She told her we were lying and then when we came home she was really angry. Made us stay in the cold, dark garden shed for a week. Please sir, don't say anything. It will only hurt us and Sam can't take the cold in the garden shed again, it will hurt her legs. Please sir."

The monk stopped and looked tenderly at Jake. He knew the boy was right and he would put it away for now. But he was not going to forget what he had heard.

"I suppose you are right, Jake, but I know I can help you a bit right now. Come to my workshop and first I will give you breakfast and then we will take a look at that hand."

The children followed Brother Godric into the workshop. They had always been curious about it and now they had a chance to see inside.

Entering the small arched door, they could see that the room was bright and cheery, lit by a roaring fire. In front of the fireplace was a comfy chair with a pile of pillows and a table beside it. On one side of the fireplace stood a shelf full of books, and on the other was a work table covered with papers and maps and diagrams. On a small shelf in one corner stood a statue of the Holy Mother with a candle in front, and a place for the monk to kneel and pray. There was a cooker, a shelf for food and dishes and rafters full of drying herbs. All in all the room was cozy but not very tidy, as there were bits and pieces lying around, papers that had been written on, old flowerpots, bits of machinery, a garden hoe; interesting things, not just sloppy things like The Bottom's.

"Pull those boxes over to the fire, children, and keep warm while I make you a little breakfast," said Brother Godric as he began moving pots and pans around. "I'm going to give you a proper English breakfast: eggs, bacon, tomatoes, mushrooms, toast dripping with honey, and a nice cup of tea. Most of it right from my abbey garden. Did you know that I have a chicken outside that lays eggs for me and bees that make honey? The tomatoes and mushrooms are from my garden. I do have to use my rations for the bacon though."

The children sat quietly and took long deep sniffs of the breakfast smells coming from the monk's cooker. It was the best thing they had smelled in a long time. Fulham was sniffing too and wiggling in Jake's pocket. When the breakfast was ready they helped Brother Godric carry it to the table. They tried to have manners and not just stuff the food in their mouths; a few times Brother Godric had to remind them to slow down. Every bite tasted so good; it was such a lovely, warm breakfast taste.

Fulham stuck his head out of Jake's pocket, making clucking noises that he too was hungry. Jake gave him a small piece of his bacon and a corner of his toast.

"NO, NO," said Brother Godric. "I didn't cook breakfast for a scruffy ferret and Miss Bottomley's at that. He probably gets more than you do to eat."

"Please Brother, he is hungry too. Can't he just have a tiny bit?"

"He would probably kill my chickens if he had half a chance," said the monk. "But I'll make you deal. If you let me see that burnt hand of yours, you can give him whatever he wants."

27

Jake hesitated, but knowing that Fulham was hungry, agreed to let Brother Godric examine his hand.

The monk held Jake's hand gently in his own and then got up and went over to his rows of books. He took one from the shelf titled, *Medicines of Pevensey Abbey* and began to leaf through it. Then he went to the work table where he began to mix things together.

"You know those old monks knew how to do quite a few things hundreds of years ago. We are lucky that they wrote down what they knew. This is oil of lavender; they used it on burns. Let me put some on your hand."

Brother Godric carefully put the paste he had made on Jake's blistered skin and then wrapped his hand in a clean white cloth. Jake could feel the pain easing right away and a sweet coolness covering his skin. He was very grateful to Brother Godric.

The monk packed apples, bread and cheese in a bag. "This will be your lunch. You had better run into the schoolroom. I can hear your teacher getting things ready. Go on now. Put Fulham in your pocket, Jake."

The children finished the last crumbs of their

breakfast, took their dishes to the sink and gathered their books. They thanked Brother Godric and entered the classroom through the little door. This was the first time since they had been in school in Pevensey that they didn't feel hungry. They were warm and fed and ready to learn.

The monk watched them go, his face troubled.

Chapter 3

A HORRID WOMAN

The school day ended at three o'clock, just as it always did. Jake and Sam put their books together slowly. They knew they could not go home yet. Miss Bottomley had told them to stay away until darkness fell. To pass the time they decided to play in the abandoned abbey where Fulham could get some exercise. He had slept in Jake's pocket almost the whole day.

"It is good ferrets like to sleep," thought Jake. "What would I have done if Fulham had awakened and disturbed the class?"

The children followed the abbey wall until they

30

came to the entrance by the old gate house. Hundreds of years ago the abbey had been a place where monks lived. They had a farm, orchards, a school and a hospital. They lived together here; they worked and prayed here, for they had dedicated their lives to God. They were known for helping the poor, giving travellers a place to stay, and nursing the sick. But then King Henry VIII came along and demanded certain things; if the monks didn't agree, they were tossed out and their abbey destroyed. That is what happened to the Abbey of Our Lady at Pevensey. What little that was left still stood proudly as a symbol of what used to be. The children liked to explore the old ruins. The site of the kitchen was easy to spot as the big chimneys still remained. They often played here when The Bottom wouldn't let them return home. They pretended they were preparing a big feast for the king; turkeys, pheasants, chickens, lovely potatoes and many sweet puddings would be served. It was fun just to pretend about food when they weren't getting any from Miss Bottomley. Today they would play hide and seek, hiding behind the walls of roofless rooms, dodging between the columns of what was left of the church and then chasing each other around the garden. Fulham followed, making clicking noises of delight and once in awhile jumping on Jake's shoulder. It was even more fun today because they were not hungry as they usually were. Brother Godric's lunch had taken care of that.

The abbey looked like this.

Brother Godric smiled as he watched Jake and Sam explore the abbey ruins. He was pleased that the children were finding a time to be real children, away from Hitler and his bombs and Miss Bottomley and her cruel ways. He was pleased his old abbey, as he had come to think of it, was a place they could do this.

When dusk began to fall, Jake and Sam made their way back to Miss Bottomley's at the edge of the village. As they approached the house, Jake took off the bandage that Brother Godric had made for him. If The Bottom saw his hand bandaged, she would know that he had talked to someone. "Better just be quiet about this," he said to Sam.

As they entered the house they could see Miss Bottomley sitting in a chair by the fire. She was shoveling spoonfuls of ice cream from an enormous bowl into her mouth. Sam stood in wonder at how fast she could shovel and how wide she could open her mouth. She was wearing glasses to read the paper. She only needed glasses for reading; when she was not reading they hung by a cord from her neck. When she was eating, food would sometimes fall from her mouth and get stuck on them. Today there were strands of spaghetti that she had had for lunch hanging from the rims and blobs of cheese sauce on the lenses and now, ice cream spots too. She was still in her night dress and had not even brushed her teeth or combed her hair since they had left that morning.

"So you stupid little brats are finally back," she said. "Hurry up in here, I have work for you to do. Jake, you go out and cut more wood for the fire. Sam, I want you to scrub this kitchen floor. I don't care if it does hurt your legs. If you do your chores well enough, maybe I will let you see what came in the post for you today."

"Oh, please tell us what it is, Miss Bottomley," said Sam "Please! We will do whatever you want us to do. Please, Miss Bottomley," pleaded Sam.

"No," said Miss Bottomley. "You work for it. Where is my sweetie, Fulham? I hope he bit your toes today."

Jake pulled Fulham out of his pocket and handed him to Miss Bottomley. As soon as she tried to take him, he jumped from her hands and ran for his cage. "Good for you, Fulham," thought Jake . "Smart one you are, to stay away from The Bottom."

"Don't just stand there," Miss Bottomley screamed at Jake. "Get moving, quickly."

Jake and Sam hurried to do what was asked of them. They did so want to see what came in the post. Perhaps it was a letter from their Mum and Dad. They had not heard from their parents since they left London and were very worried. They were desperate to know how they were, how Whidbey was, how their Nanna was. But even though they worked as best they could and as quickly as they could, Miss Bottomley made Jake cut more wood and Sam scrub the floor twice. When the wood was cut and the floors scrubbed, Miss Bottomley called them to the fireside.

From a pile of papers she pulled out an envelope that Jake could see had his mother's handwriting on it.

"It's a letter from your Mum and Dad," she said with a smile. "You know," she said slowly, "they would be so disappointed to know about your behavior and what little brats you have been. You really don't deserve to see this letter or to have the money that is in it." And she took the money from the envelope and put it under her dress, between her great breasts, and then threw the letter in the fire. "Perhaps that will teach you something," she said, picking up her paper and plopping her big bottom back into her chair.

Jake's body went rigid. He could see the letter

being burnt by the wood he had just cut. Losing control, he made a lunge for Miss Bottomley. "You have no right to do that," he said. "You are the meanest person I have ever known. Someday my parents will know about you."

Miss Bottomley grabbed him by his hair. "All right. You think you can do this to me? The only woman in the village who would take you in? I have had enough. Tonight you will have no dinner and you will both sleep in the garden shed. Out with you," she yelled, pushing them out into the cold dark night.

As the children made their way through the snow toward the garden shed, they could see Fulham pacing in his cage. His back was humped and he was hissing. He knew something was terribly wrong with his friends.

Chapter 4

THE GARDEN SHED

The tiny shed was full of Miss Bottomley's junk: old clay pots, bags of fertilizer, rakes, hoes, jars, tins, various bits of paper, a lawn mower and a garden hat.

"You'd think that The Bottom was a master gardener," said Jake, "with all this stuff about. But from the look of her garden, I'll bet she has never touched this stuff."

The shed was dark, lit only by the half light of the moon, light enough to see the spiders scurrying across the floor and the mice running under The Bottom's clay flower pots. Occasionally, the searchlights that were looking for enemy planes would reflect in the shed, reminding the children that the country really was at war.

"They are looking for the Gerries that could be on their way to bomb London," said Sam. "I hope Mum and Dad are safe. And Whidbey, too. I'm scared Jake."

"The boys in the Royal Air Force will get them," Jake assured her. "They are far better than Hitler's chicken flyers."

Throughout the night a blustery wind blew through the cracks of the thin wooden walls. The children huddled together to try to keep warm. They had no coats or blankets, but they did have what no one, not even Miss Bottomley, could take away from them, spirit and spunk! During the night when they couldn't sleep because they were so cold and uncomfortable, they whistled, sang and told jokes about Miss Bottomley. They sang:

> *Whistle While You Work*
> *Hitler is a Jerk*
> *Mussolini is a Weenie*
> *Whistle While You Work!*

And they sang *Dearest Daddy* and *Run. Rabbit. Run.* When they didn't know all the words they whistled.

"Sam," said Jake, "imagine Miss Bottomley if she had to eat what we do. She would look like a dried up prune, a football without any air. Her dresses would be too big and they would fall right off and so would her knickers. Her cheeks would be sunken in." Sam laughed hard just thinking about it.

"Or," said Sam, "think what Whidbey would do to her if he could. He would run round and round her until she would melt just like the witch in the *Wizard of Oz.* Poof, no more of The Bottom!"

The children laughed at each other's jokes for a long time. It helped them forget, for at least a little while, how cold and hungry they were. It helped them forget there was a war on.

When morning came Miss Bottomley yelled at them from the kitchen door; you wouldn't catch her out in that cold.

"Come on, get going to school so I don't have to look at you all day," she screamed.

The children, stiff and shivering, shuffled back to the house and got their coats and books without having even a moment by the warm fire.

"You go, too," The Bottom said to Fulham. "I don't want to hear your hissing all day, you little rodent."

And so, once more, the children walked to school without breakfast, passing the village bakery along the way and longing to sink their teeth into one of the lovely gingercakes in the window.

However, this morning Brother Godric was waiting for them and had a nice hot breakfast ready and a packed lunch too.

"Come on in," he called to them as he saw the children come through the school gate.

Gratefully, Jake and Sam entered Brother Godric's workshop and hurried to the fire.

"By all that is sacred you two look worse than you did yesterday! What happened last night? I want to know right now," he said, as he brought breakfast to the table.

Sam, as usual, told all, even though Jake kept making faces at her to keep quiet.

Brother Godric listened, his face growing sterner as Sam told about the letter, no dinner and the night in the shed.

"And did she tend to your hand, Jake?"

"No, Brother Godric. I took off the bandage before we got home. If she would ever find out that you helped us, she would be so angry and I'm afraid our life would be worse than it already is," Jake said, helping himself to the honeyed toast that Brother Godric had put before him.

"Give me that hand now. I'll wrap it again," said the monk. "You can eat with one hand for a bit and I'll feed Fulham his breakfast, even though he still doesn't smell like daisies."

"You know," he said, as he put a few drops of lavender oil on Jake's still tender hand, "we could do something about letters from here. We could write your Mum and Dad and tell them to send the mail here and I would give it to you."

"But we don't have money for the post," said Jake. "She took all our money."

"She sure did," Sam said, "stuck it right down her dress. We will never see it now, it is gone forever in there."

"Let me think about the post money," said Brother Godric. "I might be able to help."

And so the children and Fulham ate a great and proper English breakfast and the terror of the night before faded a bit with the bites. While they filled their mouths with good, solid food, Brother Godric told them stories about his beloved old abbey.

"For almost four hundred years this abbey was very important indeed. The church was an especially grand one and people came from all over to see it. And they came to be educated by the learned monks and they came to be made well by the monks who knew so much about medicine. Kings came here, queens, knights, ladies-in-waiting, poor people, rich people, children, old people, saints and sinners. People who were being chased, either because they really were criminals or someone thought they were criminals, would run here for shelter. There are so many stories: lepers being cured here, people hiding treasure, people falling in love here, people being made king here."

"The monks in those days were rather like you," said Sam, "helping people who need help. Like us."

"Well I suppose you could say that," said Brother Godric, "although I am certain they were a lot holier than this old monk will ever be. Look here," he said, rummaging through the papers on his desk, "this is a map of Our Lady of Pevensey Abbey as it was in the year 1345."

"Here is where the church was and this is where the monks slept. They ate here in what they called 'the refectory'. This," he said pointing to a larger spot on the map, "is the Chapter House where they met to talk about important matters and here is the treasury."

"Why did they need a treasury?" asked Jake, reaching for another piece of honeyed toast, "I thought monks were poor."

"They were," said Brother Godric, "at least, each one was poor, because they had vowed to God that they would live for Him and not for money. The monastery itself had a great deal of money."

"How did they get it?" asked Jake.

"Oh, they had fine farms and orchards and many people gave them gold or jewels so they could do the good things that they did; run their hospitals and schools and help the poor. Sometimes the monastery was rich and sometimes it was poor."

"Was it rich when the king took it?" asked Jake.

"Some say it was," said Brother Godric. "Some say it was very, very, very rich."

"Did the king take all the money," asked Sam, "like Miss Bottomley takes all the money?"

"He took a great deal of it. There is a legend though, that some of it was saved."

"What's a legend?" asked Sam, pulling herself up

stiffly from the table.

"A legend? A legend is a story that many people have told for a long, long time. It may or may not be true," answered Brother Godric, as he began to clear the table. "I'll be gobsmacked! Look at this, I won't even have to wash these plates," said Brother Godric with a smile, "you've licked them clean."

"Tell us the legend," begged Jake.

"One day I will," said Brother Godric, "but not today. I can hear your teacher getting ready for school. You had better carry on now and get in there. Take your lunch. I'm afraid it's not much today, just an egg and an apple."

"It's more than we got from Miss Bottomley," said Jake, gathering his books quickly. "Thank you for breakfast, Brother Godric. Sam is right, you are like the monks of old who used to live here and we are glad of that. Come on, Fulham, jump in," he said to the ferret. "Time for you to get your sleep."

Chapter 5

A CHANCE MEETING

Brother Godric closed the door softly after the children and sat at his work table to begin his day's work of sorting herbs and ointments and organizing things that needed tending to in the old abbey. But he couldn't keep his mind on his work. He kept thinking about Jake and Sam and that horrid Miss Bottomley.

"No use just sitting here thinking about it," he said to himself. "I have to do something." He walked over to a brown wooden box near the fireplace, opened it, and took out a small jar with a few coins in it.

"It isn't much," he thought, "but it will buy a few

stamps. Then I'm going to pay a visit to Miss Bottomley."

He put on his rumpled coat, left his workshop and made his way to the high street. A strange sight he was, a huge man with a big round face and now, with a hat that had a beak and flaps over the ears. He was almost bald; a few wisps of hair were all that remained on the top of his head. When he smiled his blue eyes twinkled and a deep and contagious laugh poured out in great pools of joy.

He made his way to the post office and purchased five stamps, chatted with the postmistress a bit, and left, heading for Miss Bottomley's cottage. He didn't have to go that far though; as he walked down the high street he spotted her peering in the bakery window. It wasn't hard to miss her as she had quite a great bottom and quite a great top. She was licking her chops over the sticky buns, egg custard tarts, biscuits and gingerbread boys. As Brother Godric approached she was sticking her hand down between her great bosoms and bringing out Jake and Sam's money. When she saw him, she quickly stuffed it back in.

"Why hello, Brother Godric," she smiled, revealing

her purple gums that matched her purple lipstick.

"Why hello to you, Miss Bottomley, how nice to see you. I was just on my way to your house."

"Oh yes," said Miss Bottomley adjusting her purple blouse so that the money would not show. "Coming to see me, Brother Godric? My whatever for?"

"I have met the evacuees who are living with you. Good little things aren't they, and smart too."

"Oh yes, they are such darlins. Don't know what I would do without them," she said, trying to smile.

"You were awfully kind to take them in," said Brother Godric, "a woman all alone like you."

"Why, yes it is a bit difficult for me," answered the awful Bottom, "but I do what I can."

"I'm sure your fine cooking will keep those children growing," he said. "I'll be watching for that."

"Oh yes, they will grow as fast as the bracken," said Miss Bottomley. "You know, Brother Godric," she said. "it is so awful, they never hear from their parents. They have been so neglected."

"Is that so?" said the monk as he watched the woman lie through her purple teeth. "Well we shall have to see that they aren't neglected while they are here in Pevensey. I am sure you will do your part."

"Oh, but of course," she answered. "I will do my part."

"I am sure you will," said Brother Godric as he looked at her closely, right into her beady eyes.

"Good day to you now, Miss Bottomley. It was nice running into you." And he walked on down the street knowing he had gotten his message across to The Bottom, that she knew someone would be watching out for Jake and Sam. They had found a powerful friend. It would be harder for her now to neglect them. He would be watching.

Miss Bottomley walked on down the street, a bit in a muddle. "How much did he know? How much had they told him?" She would have to be more careful for a little while at least. "We shall see how smart they really are," she said to herself.

Chapter 6

THE LEGEND

In the days that followed, Jake, Sam and Fulham were not quite as hungry as they had been. They developed the tasty habit of sharing breakfast with Brother Godric, and Miss Bottomley who, knowing she was being watched, let them have two helpings of porridge and an extra potato at supper time.

Even the threat of a terrible war had lessened a bit. London had not been bombed nor England invaded. Yet, although some people were calling it a phony war, Jake and Sam were reminded daily that danger was still there. At school they practiced putting on their gas masks and running for cover in case Pevensey should be bombed. They closed The Bottom's heavy blackout curtains at night so that an enemy plane could not see light and think he had a good target. On Sundays they would watch the Home Guard as they drilled. These guards were some of the older men of the village; the younger ones were already off fighting and training. Jake particularly enjoyed watching one of the guards who was older than the others and wore purple ribbons in his hair. One Sunday the guards exploded a bomb just so everyone would know what a bomb sounded like. It was terribly loud and the man with the purple ribbons jumped higher than anyone on the village green.

Since Brother Godric supplied them with postage stamps, Jake and Sam were able to write their first letter to their Mum and Dad. Jake did not want to tell them how cruel Miss Bottomley was because they would be so worried; they had enough to worry about just now, Hitler was making sure of that.

Here is what their letter said:

Our Lady of Pevensey Abbey
34 High Street
Sussex
21-3-40

Dear Mum and Dad,

Sam and I are here in Pevensey staying with
Miss Bottomley in her cottage. We go to school
every day and very often we take Miss Bottomley's
pet ferret, Fulham. Sam is managing quite nicely
with her braces. It is very quiet in Pevensey,
sometimes we miss all the noise of London and we
miss you awfully! We have found a new friend,
Brother Godric. He is a very good cook. It is better
if you send our letters to him and he will give
them to us. His workshop is right next to our
school. Please send letters to the address at the
top and please send them often because we are
desperate for mail.

Sam has received good marks in school and so
have I, except for drawing which I am not too
good at.

Love,
Jake and Sam

And so Jake and Sam received regular letters from their Mum and Dad which, once in awhile, had a bit of money tucked inside. Now, if they were very hungry they could stop at the greengrocer and buy an apple or sometimes a lardy cake at the bakery. Miss Bottomley, who didn't know what was going on and missed the money, would often tease them.

"Your parents must not love you," she would say. "They never write you. Of course I wouldn't write you either, you are such a hopeless lot. Not good for anything. Your parents don't love you," she would sing. "Ha, ha, ha and neither do I."

Sam and Jake would not reply, only keep very silent and smile inside. The secret post of Pevensey Abbey was something that The Bottom did not need to know about.

It was during this more pleasant time that one morning during breakfast Brother Godric told the children the legend of *Our Lady of Pevensey Abbey*. They had been asking him about it for some time

"I'll give it a go," he said, as he tended the fire. "Hope I can remember it all. Lets see. *The Legend of Our Lady of Pevensey Abbey...* it seems to me it starts in London at the time of King Henry VIII, somewhere

around 1532. Do you know where St. James's Park is in London?"

"I do," said Jake. "Our Nanna used to take us there; it is right close to Buckingham Palace. There are pelicans, and oh so many ducks, and a man who sells lollies. I liked going there with Nanna."

"It wasn't always as nice as that," said Brother Godric.

"During the time of King Henry it was a leper colony."

"What is that?" asked Sam

"Oh Sam," said Brother Godric, "back in those days there was a terrible disease. It hurt children as well as adults."

"Like polio hurt me?" asked Sam.

"Yes" said Brother Godric, as he looked kindly at Sam and poured himself a cup of tea, "but it was different than that. It was called leprosy and it attacked the skin and nerves. It got worse, parts of your body would begin to decay and fall off and most people who had it also became blind. There was no cure and it was a very contagious disease. People were afraid of anyone who had it, afraid that they would get it too. So if you had leprosy you had to go off and live by yourself. Usually most lepers, that's what people called them, lived together in a leper colony and in King Henry's time St. James's Park was a leper colony."

"Can you still get that disease today?" asked Jake.

"Yes, you can," said Brother Godric, "but it is rare now and curable. We don't have to worry about it at all anymore. Then it was very, very sad. If you got it you had to leave your family and friends, you had to carry a bell that you rang to let other people know you were a leper so that they could get away, and you had to find some way of getting money to feed and clothe yourself. That is why many of the lepers lived together, so they could help one another. In St. James's Park they had built little huts for one another and a sort of hospital and had a garden and a few cows and even a chapel. The stronger ones helped the weaker ones. Occasionally some good people from the town would leave them food or other things they needed but they had to leave it at the edge of the colony for fear of getting near the lepers."

"According to the legend there was a leper in the colony, a young boy by the name of Bede. I suppose he was about thirteen or fourteen. He had not had the disease very long so he was still rather strong, strong enough to help the others. And that is what he did. It was Bede who made sure there was enough water and food for everyone, nursed those who were very ill and helped organize what money they had. Of course all the lepers in the colony loved him."

As Jake listened intently to Brother Godric he watched Fulham jump up into the monk's lap. Brother Godric began to pet him and continued with the story. Jake smiled to see how fond of Fulham Brother Godric had become. He knew that would happen; it happened to most everyone.

"One day," said Brother Godric going on with the story, "one of the King's soldiers rode to the edge of the colony and made a big announcement. The King wanted the land that the leper colony used for his own hunting ground. All the lepers would have to leave within ten days. Well, of course Bede and all the other lepers were very upset. Where would they go? How would they find food and shelter? Who would nurse the sick ones?"

"Now Bede had a lot of spirit and he was quite stubborn," said Brother Godric, as he walked over to tend the fire. 'No' Bede said to the others, 'we won't go. They can't make us leave our houses, our gardens, our hospital. NO! Besides they won't come and make us move because they don't want to get near us. We can use our disease as a defense.' "

"Bede is right," said the other lepers. "They won't get near us; we shall just stay."

"And so ten days passed and the King sent another messenger telling the lepers to leave. Again they refused. Now, in those days," said Brother Godric "you did what the King said or else."

"Or else what?" asked Sam.

"Or else you got thrown in the dungeon, or put in the Tower, or had your head cut off," said Jake. He was old enough to know a little bit about history.

"That is even worse than what The Bottom does," said Sam. "But then what happened?" she asked.

"I would like to tell you the rest but it is time for school now."

"Will you tell us the rest this afternoon?" asked Jake. "The Bottom doesn't want us home anyway. We could meet you in the abbey."

Putting Fulham back in Jake's pocket, Brother Godric said, "I suppose that could be arranged. Go on now and study hard."

Chapter 7

THE TREASURE

That afternoon was a fine one, bright sunshine, blue sky, and a soft breeze carrying a faint smell of the coming spring. The children waited in the Chapter House of the old Abbey. Here they could sit on what was left of the stone chairs and enjoy the sunshine with Fulham. Presently they could see Brother Godric approaching, carrying a basket full of goodies for afternoon tea: fruit, sandwiches, scones, cream and of course, tea.

"Hurry, Brother Godric," said Sam limping up to him. "We want to hear the rest of the story."

"Yes, yes," said Brother Godric. "Hold on a

moment now and let me set up the tea!"

"Let me see, where was I?" he said, as he took the goodies from his basket.

"The lepers were told to leave," said Jake, "and Bede said 'No'."

"Oh yes," said Brother Godric "and you don't say 'No' to a king. By the way, where is Fulham?"

"Just over here," said Sam, "behind me."

" Good," said Brother Godric, "you don't want to lose sight of him here. There are so many places to get lost. I have even gotten lost in here at times. Mind him now, don't let him wander off."

"The lepers," said Sam, reminding him again.

"Oh yes. Well, when the King heard that the lepers had refused again he was royally angry and some people say he sent his soldiers to set fire to their little village. He was determined to get those lepers out, one way or the other."

"It was more than awful. The fire swept through the little village destroying the huts, the hospital, the church, and the fields and their crops. Of course the lepers had to run and the poor things didn't even know in what direction to go; some of them were too weak to run. It was Bede who organized them, led them out of the fire, got them out on the road and protected the treasure."

"Treasure? What treasure?" asked both the children together.

"Oh, did I forget to mention that?" asked Brother Godric.

"Well you see there were a few ways that the lepers came by money; sometimes the lepers' families would leave money for them, some lepers were rich anyway, or the village sold some of its farm products. Since they all wanted to help each other, they put all that they had in one place and used it when necessary. At the time of the fire they had quite a lot, no one knows how much, but the legend has come to call it a treasure."

"Where did they go then?" asked Jake , as he took an egg and cress sandwich that Brother Godric had passed to him.

"Bede had heard that the monks at Pevensey Abbey took care of lepers, so they headed here. They finally made it but I don't know how," said Brother Godric. "It was a long journey and with so many weak people it must have been very difficult, but they made it and indeed the monks did take care of them, as best they could. But that wasn't the end of the lepers' troubles."

"Old King Henry had taken their land and was using it for his hunting ground, yet that wasn't enough for him. He was also mad at all the monks in England and decided to take their abbeys too. And you know what happened when a King said he wanted something."

"You didn't say 'no'," answered Sam.

"That's right. The monks at Pevensey tried to say 'no' but that didn't work. The King's soldiers came to Pevensey Abbey. They took all that was valuable, ripped off the roof, smashed the beautiful windows, tore out the bells, kicked the monks out, left the place just like you see it today; just a shell of what it used to be."

"What happened to Bede and the lepers?" the children asked.

"The King's men scattered them all around the countryside, wouldn't let them stay together. The strange thing is no one knows what happened to the treasure. Some say Bede got away with it again and started a new colony while others say he buried it here in a very secret place. To this day it has never been found ."

"By George," said Jake, "the treasure could really be here."

"Well Jake, I think if it were here someone would have found it already. All of this happened over 400 years ago. No, I don't think it is here," said Brother Godric. "And besides, it is only a legend. It may not be true."

"You never know," said Sam thoughtfully. "It is a good story, though," she said as she watched Fulham run behind one of the old stone pillars.

The quiet of the pleasant afternoon was suddenly broken by the sound of aeroplanes overhead, many aeroplanes. It was the Royal Air Force taking off from the base that was close by Pevensey. They were flying Spitfires, fast and low.

"Go Mates!" yelled Jake, running across the wide expanse of grass where the church once stood. "Take down Hitler's planes! Keep them out of London, go boys. Take care of me Mum and Dad. Hit those Germans hard!"

"God bless and keep you safe," whispered Brother Godric as he shielded his eyes from the afternoon sun and watched the planes flying east in formation.

The three watched the sky until all the planes had

vanished into the horizon. Their minds and hearts were with those pilots, the legend of Pevensey forgotten, as the reality of wartime came back to them all.

"Time to get on home now," sighed Brother Godric. "You must go see The Bottom. Look, you have me calling her that now! Gather up Fulham. Where is he?"

"He was here just a moment ago," said Sam, "right there behind the column."

"Fulham, Fulham," she called, looking in the direction where she had last seen him. "Come on now, we must leave, it is getting late."

But there was no sign of their lively friend.

"Didn't I tell you to watch him?" scolded Brother Godric. "He could be anywhere. Oh dear, we do have a problem."

"The sound of the planes probably frightened him," said Jake. "He probably dove down a hole to get away from them. He's awfully good at that. Look around and see if you can find a hole."

"Let's all look in a different direction," said Brother Godric. "But we'd better move fast, it is getting dark and we won't be able to find him then."

"And I don't like the idea of going home without him. The Bottom would never forgive us, never." said Sam.

"Fulham, Fulham," they called.

"Sssh," said Jake. "Did you hear that?"

"What?" asked Sam

"That scraping sound. It 's coming from over there," he said as he moved to the outside wall of the Chapter House. Just as he came to the origin of the sound, out popped Fulham from a hole at the base of the wall. He ran to Jake and scampered around his feet until Jake picked him up.

"Well there you are boy, You look happy that we found you but not as happy as we are. You should not go missing like that," Jake said, patting Fulham's shiny coat.

"I know ferrets love to find rabbit tunnels," said Sam, looking at the animal closely, "but it isn't proper for you to go where we can't see you. Understand?"

"One crisis over," sighed Brother Godric. "Off with the three of you, hurry before The Bottom comes looking for you in a fit of anger."

The children did not need to be warned about Miss Bottomley's temper. They knew it well. They said their goodbyes to Brother Godric and ran for the cottage at the end of the village, Fulham in their pocket.

Chapter 8

NASTY TRICKS

After the day that Miss Bottomely met Brother Godric outside the bakery, she used many of her mean and nasty tricks just to see how smart the children really were. When it was dinner time sometimes she would say, "We shall have roasted Sam with Yorkshire pudding. Pick her up, Jake, I'll get the roasting pan."

"Act scared," Jake would whisper to Sam. "That is what she wants."

"I don't have to act," Sam would whisper back. "I am scared," and she would begin to cry.

"Come on now," The Bottom would say, "we will

need a good fire." She would wait until Sam was crying good and hard and then she would say, "Oh drat, why couldn't I have picked a tasty one. You would taste just like rubbish and with two bad legs it wouldn't be worth cooking you. We will just have cabbage and wait for you to fatten up." And she would smile and think to herself, "They are so dumb, I don't know why that Brother Godric thinks they are so smart."

She had other tricks too. For instance, she would gather up dead crickets and wrap them in crinkly paper and put them under their pillows. When the children started to go to bed she would say in a fake sweet voice, "Oh, dear little ones, tonight is the night that the fairies come to good children and leave sweets in their bed. Maybe you will get some." The children would quickly go up the stairs and get under their blankets and would feel the crinkly paper.

Sam would always think that maybe The Bottom had become kind and would say, "Oh, Jake, I hear the wrapping on the sweets, maybe the fairies have really come."

"Don't trust her Sam and whatever you do, don't eat anything," Jake would say. "Just pretend that you are delighted the fairies haven't forgotten us."

So Sam would squeal with delight so that The Bottom could hear her and Jake would quietly go to the window and by moonlight, he would unwrap the crinkly paper to see what was inside. When he found they were dead crickets he would throw them out the window but being so smart, he would keep the crinkle paper so that in the morning he could throw it in the fire and The Bottom would think they had eaten the dead crickets. She would always cackle a nasty laugh whenever she played that trick and say, "Oh, the fairies came, did they now?"

"Yes," Jake would say, "and they brought us the best candy, so crunchy and delicious." And to himself he would think, "She isn't nearly as smart as she thinks she is."

The Bottom had many more tricks: live worms in their cabbage soup, green eggs on St. Patrick's Day, and sometimes she would even throw their schoolwork into the fire and they would have to do it over.

Jake and Sam had their own tricks too. They discovered that if they complimented The Bottom she would most always become softer.

Jake would say, "Oh, Miss Bottomley you look so lovely in purple. You should wear it more often, it looks so good with your red hair."

"Do you think so, Jake?" she would answer and then give him a wee bit more food at dinner time. The compliment trick worked every time.

As did the flower trick. Sometimes on their way home from school the children would gather flowers for The Bottom. They always put a wild lily in the center so that when she put her long nose into the bouquet to smell the flowers she would get the flower dust all over her nose. Worked every time. And since she hardly ever washed or looked in the mirror, she would walk around the village for days with a golden nose.

And so the children's days passed in the village of Pevensey; not always good days but at least they were safe from Hitler, they had found a good friend in Brother Godric and thanks to him they were getting a proper English breakfast every morning and regular letters from their parents, and they had learned to at least know the tricks of the horrid Bottom.

It was late in the spring when something strange happened.

Chapter 9

FULHAM'S FIND

It was one of those wonderful late spring days with sun shining, blue, blue skies, apple and cherry trees in bloom, daffodils dotting the landscape, fields and meadows full of yellow, red and white wild flowers. When school was over in the afternoon, Jake and Sam went straight away out the door and down the street to the old abbey grounds. By now they had become quite familiar with the entire area and had explored it high and low.

As usual, Fulham was with them and was scampering around, enjoying his freedom, diving into any hole he could find and then popping up out the other side.

Ferrets are rat catchers and rabbit catchers too. They dive down the rat's hole and either catch him inside or as he tries to escape. Fulham however was a bit slow in catching things and much preferred just to go in and out the tunnels, besides there didn't seem to be much to catch in the abbey grounds. The children no longer worried that they might lose him. Normally he would appear at the tunnel's other end and run to them in delight, clucking his happy sound. But this day was different.

Jake, Sam and Fulham were playing outside the wall of what was left of the old abbey kitchen. Fulham had disappeared down a hole and Jake was sitting down with his back against the wall waiting for him to reappear. He watched the hole for a good long time but Fulham did not appear. Patiently, Jake began to whistle for him. There was no Fulham.

"Come on Fulham, I know you are in there," said Jake, looking down the hole.

Presently Jake heard the strange scraping sound, a sound of digging. Slowly, Fulham appeared and ran onto Jake's lap. As Jake began to pet him, he noticed Fulham was carrying something in his mouth. Ferrets love to steal little things and they like bright things the best.

"Let's see what you have there, Fulham," said Jake, trying to open the ferret's mouth. Fulham began to hiss and the hair on his back went straight up. He wasn't going to give up his treasure.

"I've got an idea," said Jake. "I'll trade you this apple core for what is in your mouth."

That was too much for Fulham; he dropped what was in his mouth and ran for the apple core and Jake quickly picked up the stolen loot.

It was a small piece of metal with a picture of a man and some words that Jake could not understand. He couldn't tell what kind of metal it was for it was dirty with a greenish cast. Some parts of it, however, were slightly bright. That is probably what had attracted Fulham. Jake turned it over in his hand and did not think much of it. Almost looks like an old sweet wrapper, he thought, only heavier and stronger.

"What are you two doing?" asked Sam, poking her head through what was left of an abbey window.

"Fulham just crawled out of that hole with this," Jake said.

"Let me see," said Sam.

"I think it is just a sweet wrapper," said Jake.

"Fulham would probably rather have the sweet."

"I don't know," said Sam examining it very closely, "feels more like a coin to me. What is this writing here? I can't read it."

"Neither can I," said Jake, "it seems like another language."

And then Fulham finished his apple core and straight away went down the hole again.

"Perhaps he is in there after the sweet," said Jake. "We know that animal likes to eat."

Presently Fulham reappeared and again he carried something in his mouth and ran right to Jake as if to say, "What will you trade me for this time?"

"You are a right little dodger," said Jake with a smile. "How about a biscuit crumb?" he said as he held it out to Fulham.

Again Fulham dropped his find and picked up Jake's offering.

"It looks a little like the first one," he said to Sam. "Here, what do you think?"

"It isn't exactly like the first one and I am certain it is not a sweet wrapper," Sam said as she turned it over in her hand. "It is a bit heavier but it is green like the first one. Do you think we should try to clean it?"

"I'm not sure," answered Jake slowly. "Perhaps we should ask Brother Godric. "Let's see if he is at the workshop."

The two children swooped up Fulham, who was still working on his biscuit, and ran to the abbey side of Brother Godric's workshop. The arched door of the old building was standing a bit open. Jake pushed it a bit more and called, "Brother Godric, are you here.? It is Jake and Sam."

From the far side of the room came a soft sound of snoring and then Brother Godric answered. "Humph, hmmmmm, ah what did you say? Oh, it is you, children. I was just resting my eyes here a bit, they get a little tired in the afternoon, you know. Now what is it?"

"It is these," said Sam, as she held out the two things that the ferret had found. "Fulham disappeared down a hole by the old abbey kitchen and came out with them. Jake thinks they're just some old junk."

"Hold on, let me take a look," said the monk as he straightened himself in the chair and reached for his glasses. Sam put Fulham's find in Brother Godric's rough hands. He turned them over and over and looked very closely at them.

"Let's give them a bit of a wash," he said and then he carefully wet a towel and gently rubbed them. The green cast began to partially disappear and the objects began to shine. "They definitely are not junk," he said.

"See that writing right here?" Jake said as he leaned over Brother Godric's chair. "Can you read it? Sam and I could not make it out."

"Hmmm," said Brother Godric, getting up to find his magnifying glass. He rummaged through an enormous pile of gadgets, finally found it, put the coin down on his work table and peered though the old glass.

"It looks like Latin," he said, "and this one seems to have a picture of a saint or something. It is a probably a religious medal. Yes, here it says, hmmmm, what does it say? Saint, yes that's it. Saint. But this first one is harder. The last letter looks like an 'e' and the second to last looks like a 'd', then another 'e'. The first one is almost gone, hard to say what that is. As to the material. I would say it is some kind of brass."

"'Ede' said Sam slowly. "Let's see, that could be 'eddy' or 'eiddy'. Have you ever heard of a St. Eddy,

Brother Godric?" asked Sam .

"Yes, there was St. Edward the Confessor and St. Edward of Firth. I have never heard of St. Eddy but there have been so many holy people in the world there may well have been a St. Eddy. Now this part here is quite easy to read, it is in Latin."

"Can you read Latin?" asked Sam with wonder.

"Of course," said Brother Godric, with pride. "All monks must study Latin and be able to read it. It is an old language; many other languages have come from it. See it says 'ora pro nobis'. That means 'pray for us'. Altogether it says 'Saint (whatever that name is), pray for us'."

"What about the other one ?" asked Jake.

"Let's see." Brother Godric cleaned the small piece of metal gingerly. "Some kind of coin, I think," he said. " I have never seen a coin like this though, never. I don't think it is a new coin, looks old. Where did you say you found these?"

"In the tunnel that Fulham went down, by the old abbey kitchen," said Jake.

"I think you ought to show me," said Brother Godric.

"Sure, come on," Jake said, running out the door in excitement.

"Wait for me," cried Sam. "You know I can't run as fast as you can."

"I can't run as fast as he can either," said Brother Godric. "It is you and me, Sam, we make a good team. Come on, Fulham," he said to the ferret, "show us where you found these."

As they approached the spot by the kitchen Fulham again scampered down the hole as if to claim it as his own.

"This is an interesting spot," said Brother Godric. "It may be the waste disposal tunnel."

"The waste disposal tunnel? What's that?" asked the children.

"The place in the kitchen where the workers threw out the garbage," answered Brother Godric. "Most abbey kitchens had them."

"Come on back now, Fulham," Jake called, as he knelt looking down the hole. As he did that the earth around the hole gave way and became much larger.

"Cor," yelled Jake, "it almost took me with it."

"Interesting," said Brother Godric, "very interesting."

"Fulham, come on out now," said Sam, "you have been in there too long and you are beginning to worry me, you silly ferret."

Fulham did not appear.

"Come on now, Fulham," said Jake in his most commanding voice, "time to pop out."

No Fulham.

Brother Godric also called for Fulham but his manly voice didn't help either. The ferret was not responding.

"Oh my, what if he is lost down that hole?" said Sam. "The Bottom really will have me for dinner."

"Now, now," said Brother Godric, "don't worry, he will come. Just be patient."

"Sing to him, Jake," said Sam. "He likes it when you do that at night."

So Jake tried singing but that didn't help either. Fulham was being quite stubborn and determined.

Just as Jake was launching into his next song and Sam was still yelling down the hole, who should appear on the abbey green but Miss Bottomley herself.

"I was shopping on the high street and thought I heard Fulham's name. What in the world are you two doing, you nasty brats?"

Brother Godric coughed.

"Oh hello, dear Brother Godric, "she said in her

fake sweet voice. "I didn't see you there at first. What are my darlings doing?" she asked, adjusting her hat.

"It seems," said Brother Godric, "that Fulham has gone down the hole and won't come out. It is very strange."

"He'll come to me," she said. "Come on, Fulham, darling, it is your sweet Mummsey. Come out of there now."

There was no sign of Fulham.

"Come on, darlin," Miss Bottomley pleaded in her sweetest voice. "I have missed you today and I want to see you."

"Fulham surely doesn't want to see her," thought Jake. "He is probably hiding down there hoping she will go away."

"Fulham! Fulham!" yelled Miss Bottomley, her voice rising to a shriek.

Fulham still did not appear.

Miss Bottomley got down on her hands and knees to get closer to the hole. Putting her face right at the opening she pounded on the ground yelling, "Fulham, Fulham you get up here right this very instant!" And she would pound again.

With all the pounding the ground began to give way ever so slightly around the hole and then, it fell in more and more, sucking Miss Bottomley right with it, head first down into the hole, just like Alice in Wonderland, only she did not go all the way down.

She was stuck in the hole up to her waist, her big bottom sticking out, her purple stockinged legs kicking furiously, her purple knickers showing, and her purple skirt spread out on the top of the ground around the hole.

Sam and Jake and Brother Godric could not help it. They fell to the ground laughing. It was the best thing that they could have ever hoped would happen to Miss Bottomley. It was hilarious. It was super! It was the grandest! They had Miss Bottomley just where they wanted her.

But then, shortly, Brother Godric got ahold of himself and realized that she could be in real danger. She could suffocate in there, head first and all.

"Come on, children, we have to help her out."

"Do we really? Couldn't we just enjoy this moment a bit longer?" pleaded Sam, breathless from laughing.

"No, no we really must hurry, she won't last very long if she can't breath."

Reluctantly, Jake and Sam followed Brother Godric's instructions.

"Give her a good tug now," said Brother Godric as Jake and Sam each held on to Miss Bottomley's enormous legs. "I'll pull from her waist."

They pulled and pulled but The Bottom was stuck fast. The three tried again and again but nothing seemed to work.

As the pulled they could hear Miss Bottomley's muffled voice. They couldn't tell what she was saying but they could definitely hear her voice.

"Good," said Brother Godric, "she is breathing at least. She probably has a bit of air down there, that will give us more time."

"Jake," he said, "run to the village and get as many people as you can find to help. But be quick about it. If you fall down, don't take time to get up."

Jake ran to the bakery, the post office, the library, and the petrol station, not falling once. He returned with four more people, who were astonished to see The Bottom in such a predicament and who also couldn't help but laugh, even as they heard her earth-bound cries.

"Come on, mates," said Charlie, the man from the petrol station, "the six of us ought to be able to do this."

They tugged and tugged at the poor stuck body of

Miss Bottomley but she only budged the tiniest bit.

"All right now," said Charlie, "I have an idea. Jake, you lie down here on the ground so you can push Miss Bottomley's bum with your feet. That will give us a bit of leverage while we pull."

"Yes sir," said Jake with a smile he couldn't conceal and laying with his back on the ground he put his feet squarely on The Bottom's bottom.

"Okay, now push on the count of three," said Charlie. "One, two, three!" and Jake pushed as hard as he could. "This one is for scaring Sam and trying to put her in the stove," he thought.

"One, two, THREE!" came the count from Charlie. "And this one is for those nasty insects you wrapped up," Jake thought as he gave Miss Bottomley's bum another shove.

"I think it is working," said Brother Godric. "She is about to come uncorked."

"Don't give up now," said Charlie to everyone. "Try your hardest."

"Be glad to," said Jake and he kicked and pushed the purple covered bottom as hard as he could. "This," he thought, "this is for the day I burned my hand."

With a great popping noise Miss Bottomley's head

reappeared and more dirt fell from the sides of the hole and down inside. Miss Bottomley, red in the face and breathing hard, was holding Fulham by the back of his neck.

"Who was kicking me?" she demanded. "Being stuck, almost suffocating, was bad enough without someone kicking me too. Who was it?"

"The only way to get you out, dear Miss Bottomley," said Miss Gardner the librarian. "You know we all had to work together and little Jake here was doing his part, just like Charlie told him to. The boy is actually a sort of hero."

Miss Bottomley glowered at Jake as if to say, "Wait till I get you home."

Jake knew it was time for a compliment. "Oh Miss Bottomley, you were so brave. You risked your life for Fulham and look, you rescued him and he isn't hurt a bit."

"Yes, yes," agreed all the others and as they began to clap.

Miss Bottomley, her hair and face covered in dirt, said, "It was nothing. I was only looking out for my ferret. Really, nothing at all. I had to tug him a bit, he was stuck on something down there, probably why he wouldn't come out in the first place. Oh my, oh my." she said, "I need to sit down."

"I think we should all go back to my workshop to wash up and have a cup of tea," said Brother Godric as he moved everyone away from the hole. "You too, Fulham!"

And so they all went to Brother Godric's workshop and had tea and biscuits out of Brother Godric's old china cups. When Miss Bottomley began to feel a bit better she said she ought to be going, thanked all the villagers who had helped, and told the children to come along.

"Could I keep them for just a little while?" asked Brother Godric. "I need them to help me move a stone over the hole so that no one else will fall into it. We don't want two accidents in one day."

"That will be fine," said Miss Bottomley, "but I'm taking Fulham home with me. He always seems to get into trouble when he is with those children. Come along, Fulham, Mummsey will take you home," she said, ignoring Fulham's struggling to get away from her.

Chapter 10

INTERESTING DISCOVERIES AND MEAN TRICKS

As soon as Miss Bottomley was out of sight, Brother Godric turned to the children and said, "Hurry, we must get back to the hole before she, or someone else, decides to come back."

"Why the hurry, Brother Godric?" asked Sam. "Its only a hole."

"No Sam, I think it's more than that," said Brother Godric. "I think Fulham may have discovered more than that."

The three ran across the abbey green, Jake running ahead, Sam bravely trying not to fall on brace bound legs and Brother Godric holding his

robe up so as not to trip. When they reached the hole Brother Godric got down on the ground and said, "Yes, just as I thought."

"What did you think?" asked Sam. "Tell us! You are making me wild with curiosity."

"See down there, look very closely but don't fall in, be careful, the earth is loose there."

Jake and Sam both joined him on the ground and peered into the hole.

"Looks like pieces of wood," said Jake.

"Yes, almost like a floor," said Sam.

"Yes, yes," said Brother Godric, "and I wonder what is under the floor. It doesn't look like it is part of the waste disposal tunnel. I have never seen anything like this around the abbey and I am not sure what it could be. If it wasn't for Fulham getting lost and Miss Bottomley falling in, the earth would not have given way for us to find it. I saw it as we pulled out the purple Bottom," he said. "It must have made an air pocket so she could breathe, otherwise she probably wouldn't have lasted. I don't think anyone else noticed it."

"Let's go see what it is," said Jake as he began to climb into the hole.

"NO!" said Brother Godric firmly. "We must be very careful about when we do it and we must have the right equipment. Besides it's getting dark, and we won't be able to see."

"When then, Brother Godric?" asked Sam, full of excitement.

"Perhaps after school tomorrow. When you leave in the morning, tell Miss Bottomley that I need your help and you may be late. She won't mind . She is still grateful to me for pulling her out of the hole. This will give me time to look in some of my books about the abbey. I may have overlooked something."

"I can't wait to tell her," said Sam. "She will be mad that she didn't see it first."

"No, no, don't tell her yet," said Brother Godric. "I don't think it is a good idea at all, not until we really know more."

"You must promise not to tell, Sam," said Jake. "You know how you like to talk."

"I promise," said Sam solemnly. "I promise. I promise. There are you satisfied, Jake? I can keep a promise, you know that."

"This isn't the time for squabbling," admonished Brother Godric. "Help me now, we really do have to cover up this hole."

The three pushed a large block of stone that had once been part of the abbey over the hole. It looked as though it had been there for a long time when they finished, as though it was in its proper place.

"Go on now," said Brother Godric. "I told Miss Bottomley that I wouldn't be keeping you long. Hurry, I'll see you tomorrow."

And so the children hurried to the cottage at the end of the village where The Bottom waited for them. She was back to her old tricks, the sweetness she had faked for Brother Godric and the other villagers was gone, completely. She was sitting at the kitchen table surrounded by the usual dirty plates and bits and pieces of food: chicken bones, dried potatoes, burnt toast, coffee grinds and she hadn't even cleaned herself up from her fall in the hole. She was still just as dirty as when they last saw her.

"You're finally home. That must have been some rock you had to move, took you long enough, so long, my dears, that I have eaten your dinner and there is none left. If you had been here earlier, you could have had roast pork and applesauce and lovely white rolls," she said, as she picked her teeth with the end of her knife and then examined what she had retrieved. "And so, my little ones, you must get to your chores now, hungry or not. First though you must help me get this dirt off. Sam, you get a nice warm bowl of water and wash my face and, Jake, you can clean my hands and fingernails," she said stretching her filthy hands towards him.

The children looked at each other in silence and dutifully followed directions. They knew they didn't have a choice. As Jake washed The Bottom's large hands he thought, "Why didn't I give this woman a larger shove on her bottom this afternoon? One that would kick her all the way to Germany. She could live with Hitler. I'm sure she would be happier there and he would love to have her. She is just his kind."

Sam scrubbed Miss Bottomley's face so hard that she yelled at her. "You little brat, what do you think you are doing? You are going to scrub my skin off, you are."

And Sam said to herself, "That would probably be an improvement, my dear Miss Bottomley."

That was not the end of Miss Bottomley's mean and nasty tricks. When the children had finally finished all their chores and climbed the stairs up to their beds in the loft, still so very, very hungry, they discovered that Miss Bottomley had been there before them. Sam usually put the doll that she had brought from home on her pillow, but tonight, as she entered the room, she saw that her doll Emma, her precious memory of home, her only toy, was gone. Not there at all.

"What has she done? How could anyone be so cruel? Where is Emma?" screamed Sam."

"Shh," whispered Jake. "You know that is just what she wants; she wants to hear you unhappy. She is probably listening at the bottom of the steps. We have to be smarter than she is. Emma must be around here. The Bottom is too lazy to throw her in the rubbish. Look around, Sam, look around," he said as he put his arm around her.

Sam began to sob low pitiful sobs as she peered under the covers and in the corners of the room.

As Jake helped with the hunt he discovered that his teddy that he had brought from London, the one he had carried in his suitcase because he didn't want older boys to see him taking it, was also gone, just gone, disappeared.

"They aren't in this room. I have looked

everywhere. Do you think she would have thrown them out?" asked Sam as she opened the little cottage window.

Jake joined her at the window and there spot on, hanging in the branches of the tree outside their window, they could see Emma dangling dangerously by her hair on the end of a branch and Jake's teddy not far away, stuck between two big branches.

"Get them, Jake," said Sam. "Oh please get them. Please!"

But as Jake began to think about how he could do that, Sam said, "Wait, wait, wait. Look what they are next to."

There in the evening twilight, Jake could just barely see that both Emma and Teddy were hanging very close to a beehive, a big beehive.

"What a witch!" exclaimed Sam. "She put them there on purpose, thinking she could outsmart us. Well she doesn't know us very well. She doesn't know that our class at school has been studying bees and I know that if you wait until dark, the bees go to sleep and they will not even know we are near their hive. Except, of course, for the guard bees."

"Oh right," said Jake, "just a tiny little thing like the guard bees. And how do you propose to get by them, Miss Smarty, especially at night?"

"That will take some thought," pondered Sam.

"There is an old clothes pole that has been sitting under the eaves ever since we came," she said. "Let's see if it is long enough, but be quiet, The Bottom may not be asleep yet."

Quietly they took the pole and pushed it out the window, toward the tree but it was too short to reach Emma and Teddy.

"I've got a great idea," said Sam. "What if we tie one of my braces to the end of the pole with one of my hair ribbons? I think it will reach then."

"Cor, you are right," said Jake. "But we must wait until dark."

"And then we must do it ever so slowly, an inch at a time, so we don't alert the guard bees," said Sam.

So the children waited a few hours until it was very dark and they could hear the snores of The Bottom and then ever so slowly, painfully slowly, they pushed the pole and Sam's brace to the tree, past the sleeping hive and its guard bees. First they retrieved Emma and then, repeating the long process, they were able to bring Teddy back too, although they did think they had lost him several time

"Whizzo! We outsmarted her! I knew we could. I knew we would," shouted Sam, giving Emma a big hug.

"Now in the morning, act like nothing has happened, said Jake. "It will make her bonkers."

"Sam," said Jake as he settled down under the covers, "what do you think is in that hole at the abbey?"

"I don't know, but I bet Fulham does. I wish he could talk," Sam said with a yawn. "Goodnight now, Jake."

Jake didn't go right to sleep. He kept thinking about the coin with the saint's name on it. "St. Ede, such a strange name," he thought. "There was an Eddy in my class in London and there was Eddy the butcher down the street, but they didn't spell it 'Ede'. I've never heard of a St. Ede. But then it looked like there was another letter on the coin, like the first letter was rubbed off. What could it be?" he thought, as he put different letters in front of 'ede'.

"Mede? Lede? Bede? Bede's it! St. Bede! I have heard of him. Bede, the leper in *The Legend of Pevensey Abbey*, must have been named after him. It is Bede!

Wait until Brother Godric hears about this. He will be so surprised."

And Jake fell asleep holding his London teddy and dreaming about old abbeys and beehives.

Chapter 11

RIDDLES SOLVED

"Were you a little lonely last night, children? Were you missing something?" Miss Bottomley asked with a nasty laugh, when she called up the steps of the loft to wake Sam and Jake.

"Yes," said Sam, "but I think we are all right now; we still miss your lovely smile, though."

Jake rolled his eyes at Sam, she was using the compliment trick.

"I don't have a lovely smile, you know that," said The Bottom. "Me mum always said I had an ugly smile, the ugliest in the village, I am proud to say. My smile is just like me mum's."

"Oh no, Miss Bottomley," said Sam from the top of the steps, "it is a pretty smile, really."

"If I say it's ugly, it's ugly!" The Bottom roared. "Now you go on and get out of here before I have to come up there after you."

Jake and Sam tumbled down the steps, grabbed Fulham and as they ran out the door towards the high street, they called back. "We'll be late tonight, Miss Bottomley, have to help Brother Godric." Before she could object, they were halfway across the bridge that led to school. They knew it was better to leave quickly than to take a chance on The Bottom's tricks.

When they were gone, The Bottom walked towards the mirror that hung by the door and smiled slowly at herself. It was the first time she had truly looked at her smile since she was a child. It was a smile that came from deep inside her, not the fake smile that she usually used. She looked at the person in the mirror smiling back at her and liked what she saw. Maybe it wasn't an ugly smile after all, she thought. During the rest of the day she went back to the mirror several times.

While The Bottom was still smiling at herself, Jake was telling Sam what he had figured out the night before.

"I think it is Bede," he said. "St. Bede. It makes sense, doesn't it? I mean he is a saint and no other letter works with it."

"So the medal would say, *St. Bede pray, for us?*" asked Sam.

"Right," said Jake, "but let's tell Brother Godric, he will know for sure. Monks know a lot about saints."

When they arrived at Brother Godric's workshop he was busy once again making their breakfast. It had become a daily meal for the children and of course a place where they could get mail from their parents. They were eager to see what he had cooked up today and even more excited to tell the monk what they had discovered.

"Brother Godric, Brother Godric, listen," said Jake as he ran up to the stove where Brother Godric was frying up rashers. "I think I figured out the medal that Fulham found, you know, the one that says 'pray for us' on it. Is there a Saint Bede? Is there, Brother Godric? Doesn't that make sense?"

Brother Godric dropped the fork he was using and said with amazement. "Why of course that's it. Bede! I don't know why I didn't think of it and he, a monk like myself. It never entered my mind. Well done, Jake! Well done! Let's look at the medal again."

The three of them got the medal out of the special jar where Brother Godric had put it and looked at it again with Brother Godric's magnifying glass.

"It fits, it fits, "said Sam. "Look, there are very small remnants of a 'B'. It must be it."

"I think I have a book with a drawing of St. Bede," said Brother Godric and he quickly scoured through his books. Lifting an enormous book from the top shelf, he began to turn the pages carefully and thoughtfully.

While the three detectives were busy with books and magnifying glasses, Fulham was busy eating the bacon that was meant for the children's breakfast. He had lived with the The Bottom for so long that he had picked up her tricky ways.

"Here, here it is ," said Brother Godric, "right here. It is a drawing from the time; they didn't have cameras then. See, he has a beard and monk's clothing."

"What does he have in his hand?" asked Sam.

"That is a writing instrument that they used in those days," said Brother Godric.

"Let's see what the book says about him." *A priest*

and monk in the monastery of Peter and Paul. Lived 672-731 A.D. Great teacher, writer and scholar.

That's why he has the pen in his hand, " said Jake. "Read some more please, Brother Godric."

A saint greatly loved by medieval Christians, Brother Godric read thoughtfully.

Sam was examining the medal very closely, turning it over in her hands.

"Look," she said, "the man on the medal looks like the one in the book. It must be Bede. It just must be."

"I think you are right," said Brother Godric, as he too looked at the medal. "It must be Bede."

By this time Fulham had moved on to the muffins.

"Wasn't Bede the name of the leper in the *Legend of Pevensey Abbey?*" asked Jake.

"Yes," said Brother Godric, "that was his name."

"And doesn't the legend say that he came here?"

"Yes," said Brother Godric.

"Well, if he was named after St. Bede, wouldn't it make sense that he could be wearing a medal that said, *Saint Bede, pray for us?*

"Well, yes," said Brother Godric.

"Well then, maybe this medal belonged to our Bede, the leper."

"Now Jake, now Sam, don't go on. You know the story is only a legend."

"But legends sometimes have a bit of truth in them," said Jake, "you told us that yourself."

"Yes, yes I did," said Brother Godric. "But don't get too excited. I went over and over all the books about the abbey and I couldn't find anything that might explain why medals and coins would be in the waste disposal tunnel or why there is a floor at the bottom of that hole."

"Can't we still look at it after school?" asked the children.

"Oh yes, I have all that planned. I have some shovels and I'm going to put a sign on the gates saying that the abbey will be closed this afternoon. That will allow us to dig without drawing attention to ourselves."

"Maybe Fulham can help too," said Sam.

"I'm counting on that. Speaking of Fulham, where is he?"

They all turned toward the stove to see Fulham, his face covered with food and his belly so full that he could hardly walk, clucking contentedly as he began to nibble on the blueberries that Brother Godric had prepared.

"That's our breakfast!" Sam yelled at Fulham. "You ate last night, we didn't."

"Again?" cried Brother Godric. "She didn't put you to bed without any dinner again? After all the help you gave her at the hole?"

"Yes, she did," said Jake.

"And that wasn't all she did," said Sam. "She took my doll, Emma, and threw her into a tree right next to a beehive. And she threw Jake's London Teddy there too. But we got them back. We can always outsmart her."

Jake was a bit embarrassed because he really didn't want anyone but Sam to know that he even had a London Teddy.

"That woman needs some prayers," mumbled Brother Godric. "Sometimes when we use the compliment trick it works," said Sam.

"What is the compliment trick?"

"Oh we say something nice to her and for a few minutes she is nicer. Like this morning, I told her she had a lovely smile. I thought it would work but she exploded and said that she had an ugly smile, that her mum had told her that. Wouldn't it be awful to think that you had an ugly smile?"

"Well now, I think maybe you two are close to the answer. Monks have always said that it's better to treat mean people with honey than with vinegar. Maybe if you keep complimenting her, doing thoughtful things, maybe even giving her little gifts, she may change."

"But that is so hard when she is so mean," said Jake.

"I know, I know, " said Brother Godric. "But maybe it is worth a try."

"It will take an awfully long time to change that heart," said Jake.

"Come on now, forget Miss Bottomley for a moment," said Brother Godric. "Eat what Fulham left you and I will fix you eggs too. Then off to school with you. Study hard and the day will go fast. Before you know it the school day will be over and we can go explore the hole in the abbey."

That was much harder than Brother Godric made it sound. All during his lessons Jake and Sam thought of nothing else but tunnels, St. Bede, coins and the Legend of Pevensey Abbey. Once, when the teacher asked who discovered America, Jake answered, "St. Bede, sir!" It was most embarrassing.

Chapter 12

BEDE'S SPIRIT

When school was finished Jake and Sam went to the abbey as quickly as they could. They found Brother Godric all ready for them. He had several shovels and some wood to shore up the hole so that the earth would not fall in on them. As much as he tried to hide it, he was as excited as the children.

"First," he said, "we must push back the stone. We did a proper job on it last night, no one would ever know that there is a hole under there."

And so they huffed and puffed and moved the stone away from the hole. The afternoon sun was angled perfectly to shed enough light inside to make the floor more visible than it had been the night before.

Fulham sensed that he was back at his favorite tunnel and struggled to get out of Jake's pocket.

"Okay, okay," said Jake. "Out you go, Fulham, but this time you can't get too lost because I am coming with you."

"Oh no," said Brother Godric, "I'm going down there first."

"Sorry, Brother Godric," said Sam. "I think you'd better look again. The hole is not big enough for you or Jake. It's going to have to be me."

"No, no," replied Brother Godric. "You are just a little girl and I am afraid your leg braces might cause you trouble."

"I don't think so," insisted Sam. "I've got used to them. I can do almost anything,"

"She can," agreed Jake. "She does much better than I would do if I had leg braces. She is very slow and methodical, that may be just what we need."

Reluctantly Brother Godric agreed that Sam would be the first to go down the hole but before that happened they must dig more earth to make the hole bigger and cover its sides with the wood he brought.

They did that; it took quite a long time and much hard work.

"Now Sam, before you go in there you must let me tie this rope around you," said Brother Godric. "I'll hold on to the end and slowly let you down."

Sam agreed, for when she looked down the hole, she could see that it was almost ten feet to the bottom and it was too steep to crawl out; she was not going to object to the rope.

As Brother Godric and Jake began to lower her slowly down the sides of the hole, Fulham jumped out of Jake's pocket and onto Sam's shoulder. He wasn't going to miss this for anything.

"Get that blamed ferret!" said Brother Godric. "He will only cause trouble."

"Let him stay," whispered Jake. "He will give Sam courage."

"Hmmph!" answered Brother Godric. "Hmmmph!"

Sam slowly reached the bottom and as her feet hit the wooden floor they could all hear a sound of hollowness, as if the wood was just not sitting on the ground, as if there was something underneath it.

Sam stood on the wood and looked up at Jake and Brother Godric. "Now what?" she called up to them.

"Knock on the wood," said Brother Godric. Sam knocked on the wood with the bottom of her brace; the hollow sound came again but the floor didn't move.

"Is there a handle on the wood or anything that might open it?" asked Brother Godric.

"Can't see anything," said Sam.

"Hit it again with your brace," said Jake, "as hard as you can."

Sam kicked the floor as hard as she could. On the second kick, the entire floor fell in and took Sam with it.

"Yikes!" yelled Sam, as she twirled on the end of the rope, "I hope you two are still holding on, it is pretty dark here," she said, trying to hide her fear.

"We have you, we have you," assured Brother Godric. "Maybe we should pull you up now. This is getting too dangerous."

"No, no," said Sam firmly. "I am fine, really I am. It would be nice though if I had a light so I could see more."

"Send Fulham up the rope and I'll give him the one Dad gave me. He can take it back to you."

"Okay," said Sam and she gave Fulham a nudge

and told him to go to Jake. Fulham understood and ran up the rope very easily, because ferrets can do things like that. Jake searched in his pocket, gave the torch to Fulham and he took it back down to Sam.

Jake's torch was a very little one so she couldn't see everything but it did help.

"Looks like I am in a room ,"said Sam. "Yes, yes it is a room and there are shelves on the walls, lots of cobwebs. Yuck it smells so mouldy."

"How big is it?" asked Brother Godric.

"Can't tell, too dark," said Sam.

"Is there anything on the shelves?" asked Jake.

"Hard to tell," said Sam. "Maybe, wait a moment, let me look right here close to me."

She put her hand straight out into the dark; a very brave thing for anyone to do anywhere.

"Yuck!" she called. "There is a mass of cobwebs here. I hope I don't grab a spider or some other nasty thing." She felt around all over in the darkness in front of her.

"Hold on, hold on," she called. "What is this? Feels like a box but I can't see."

"Hold the rope still. I keep swinging out away from the side."

As Sam tried to feel in the darkness, Fulham got excited and jumped off her shoulder into the darkness.

"Oh my!! Fulham is gone!" screamed Sam. "I can't see him."

"Use the light," answered Jake. "Quickly!"

"Okay," said Sam and she did the best she could with that little light.

"Fulham!" she called, " Fulham come back here!" As the light hit the abbey side of the hole, she saw the end of his tail disappear into the side of the tunnel.

"Good gracious, it looks like he has found another tunnel!"

"Where?" asked Brother Godric.

"Here, over here on this side," said Sam.

"Time to come up," commanded Brother Godric. "We have to rethink this whole thing, it is getting complicated ."

"And my arms are getting tired," said Jake.

When Sam was pulled to the top and dusted off, Brother Godric gave her apple cider that he had brought in his thermos; he always thought of food and drink.

"You are so brave," he said. "Well done, well done,

Sam!"

"Well done!" added Jake, giving her a pat on the back.

"It is very exciting down there," she said. "It feels like a small room, only I really don't know because I couldn't see it all. It is hard when you are swinging on the end of a rope. I am worried about Fulham, Brother Godric."

"Me too," agreed Brother Godric. "Now, what side of the hole was it that he disappeared into?"

"There by the abbey. I just saw the end of his tail disappear."

"Hmmm, so if he went that way, it would be toward the kitchen area. Perhaps that would be where he would come out."

"Let's go look around there," said Jake. "Come on!"

The three ran into the old kitchen and felt the floor and the walls, anywhere that could hide a small opening.

"Listen," whispered Jake, "it is Fulham making his clicking sound." As they followed the sound of the noise, Fulham suddenly stuck his head out between two stones and jumped onto Jake.

"You silly ferret," cried Jake, "you do cause trouble,

you certainly do."

As Jake scolded Fulham, Brother Godric examined the hole that he came from. He pushed on one of the stones. "Look," he said, "this stone is a bit loose, probably just from being here so long."

"And so is the one under it," said Jake excitedly. "Let's see if we can pull them out. There has to be a connection between here and the hole outside or Fulham couldn't have found the way out."

As they pushed at the two stones, they actually came out quite easily. They were heavy and it took the three of them to move them, but they did move. After they moved the first two, two more were able to be moved and then still two more. The three were getting very excited.

As the next two were moved Jake said, "Look, look! It is a small door behind there."

"A secret door," yelled Sam. "A real secret door."

"Holy Bede, what have we found?" exclaimed Brother Godric.

"It must lead to the bottom of the hole," answered Sam. "Come on, let's open it. It almost looks like it is asking to be opened."

At this point Fulham was running around and

around as if to say, "open it, open it."

"All right, but carefully," said Brother Godric, "very carefully. We don't want to disturb more of the wall than we have to."

The door was about four feet high, arched at the top, made of wood that had blackened with age. There were three metal straps across it to give it strength.

Brother Godric put his hand on the latch and pulled. It didn't appear to have a lock but he could hear a click. As he pulled nothing seemed to move.

"Let us help," urged Sam. The three pulled with all their might but the door did not move.

"I remember reading a book about locks," said Jake. "Sometimes, long ago, handles were made to be very tricky. See if you can turn it Brother Godric."

Brother Godric tried but nothing happened.

"Try it the other way," suggested Jake. Brother Godric tried and they all heard a click.

"Do it again," said Sam and Jake together.

Brother Godric did as he was told and slowly, very slowly the door began to open.

They all peered inside the hole with wonder and amazement. It was indeed the room at the bottom of the hole where Sam had been, now the light from the kitchen area was permitting them to see more. Just as Sam thought, it was a room lined with shelves. On the shelves were bottles, baskets, barrels and a few metal boxes, as if things from the kitchen were stored there.

Brother Godric, Jake and Sam began carefully looking inside the bottles and baskets. They were very dusty and anything that had been inside had long since decayed.

"Probably food stored from the kitchen," mused Brother Godric. "These are definitely wine bottles. They look almost like the ones we use today and that is a beer barrel. I would know that anywhere."

"Why would they have covered the door with stones if they had to use this room for the kitchen?" asked Sam.

"I don't know," said Brother Godric. "I have been asking myself the same question."

"Look at this metal box," said Jake. "Do you think we should open it?"

"We have opened everything else," replied Sam. "Why not?"

The box was made of heavy black metal and was about as big as the small suitcase that Jake had

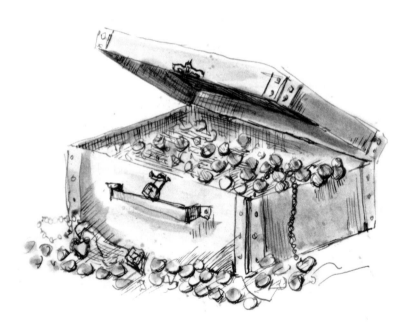

brought with him from London. It had a lock on it.

"What about the lock?" asked Jake.

"You were good with the door, what do you think?" Brother Godric asked Jake.

Jake began to examine the lock but as he did so, it fell right off into his hand. It had grown so rusty over time that the metal had worn thin.

"That looks like a sign that we were meant to open it," whispered Sam, as Jake carefully lifted the lid.

Suddenly it was very quiet in that room as the three stood in awed silence. The contents of the box glittered and shone brightly in the half light. The old metal box was brimming with gold and jewels: gold coins in small sacks, necklaces and bracelets, some with jewels, and diamonds and rubies mixed in with it all.

Brother Godric sat right down on the floor and exclaimed over and over, "What *have* we found? What *have* we found?"

Sam and Jake carefully looked at the treasure of gold coins and jewels as if they were in a dream.

"Brother Godric, Brother Godric, look there is some kind of a message here," said Jake.

"I can't read it. Can you?"

Brother Godric took the old parchment to the light of the open door, fumbled for his glasses and examined the document closely. "It is in Latin," he said breathlessly. "Let's see, it says:"

To all who read these words: he paused to take a breath. *In the year of Our Lord 1532, Henry the VIII, King of Ireland and England ruthlessly and selfishly and without compensation took the land of the lepers to be used for his own pleasure. The monks of Pevensey Abbey were kind enough to take us in, but now the King has heard of their kindness and of their reluctance to follow his new laws with regard to religion. We receive word that his soldiers are on their way to destroy Pevensey Abbey. I fear for the future of the lepers, indeed, for their very lives. In this box is the lepers' treasury. Only my friend Peter and I know where it is hidden. If someone finds this who does not know of the lepers, take some for yourself and use the rest for the sick, as was its original intent.*
I trust in your goodness. Bede

"Bede," whispered Sam. "It is from Bede."
"*The Legend of Pevensey Abbey*," shouted Jake, "isn't just a legend after all! It is true, it is true. And we

found the treasure. Wizzo!"

"I feel like Bede is almost here in the room with us, " Sam said, softly. "It is very sad that we really don't know what happened to all the lepers."

Brother Godric was still sitting on the floor with Bede's letter in his hand, stunned. Was it really true or was he just dreaming? He rose from the floor and walked over to the box and touched the coins. No, he was not dreaming, they were really there and he was truly holding a letter from Bede the Leper in his hand.

"How much do you suppose is in there?" asked Jake.

"Oh, there is lots and lots," said Brother Godric, "lots and lots, and because it is so old, it is very valuable indeed."

Fulham jumped into the box and was attempting to run off with some of the coins.

"Oh no you don't," said Sam, as she lifted him up and looked right in his face, "these are not for you."

"Now what do we do, Brother Godric?" Jake asked. "I mean what do we do? Who should we tell and where do we go with it?"

"Yes, Brother Godric, what do we do?" asked Sam.

"Do you know the mansion that sits at the top of the hill at the other end of the village?" Brother Godric asked Jake.

"Yes, you mean Lord Baker's estate?"

"The very one. You must go there now and tell Lord Baker to come quickly. He is our town's constable. Tell him I said to come and it is very urgent. Run now, as fast as you can. He must come before it gets too dark."

"And Jake," Brother Godric shouted after him, "tell him to come in the back way to the abbey. I don't want anyone to start asking questions."

Chapter 13

A SMILE REMEMBERED

Jake ran quickly through the village, hoping that no one noticed him, especially The Bottom. What he really wanted to do was to shout to all the people and tell them what they had found; he knew that wasn't a smart idea. He turned down the long driveway that led to Lord Baker's enormous house, running past the cows and the sheep that were in the adjacent fields. "I wonder if I told them what we have found, would they know what I was talking about? Probably not," he thought. "I have never seen a cow or a sheep interested in gold coins or jewels."

When he finally arrived at the house, he ran up the

long set of steps and lifted the brass knocker so that it bounced loudly on the door. When no one answered, he knocked again. Soon he could hear footsteps and, the massive door creaked opened.

"What is it, lad? What do you want?" said the tall servant who stood in the doorway. "How dare you come to this door making such a racket. Shouldn't a boy like you go to the back door?"

"Brother Godric sent me," panted Jake. "I need to see Lord Baker."

"Brother Godric? I see," said the servant. "Come in!" And he led Jake into a long, long reception hall filled with all manner of things: big urns full of walking sticks, kites, deer heads mounted on the wall, fossils, paintings of ancestors staring down from their high perch, swords, armor, clocks of various kinds, books, Wellies, dog leashes, baskets of logs and bells both small and large.

"Sit here," ordered the servant, "but please do be careful," he said, looking at Jake's dusty and rumpled clothes.

Presently a man appeared; a tall man with a head full of flyaway grey hair that strangely enough had purple ribbons in it. He wore overalls and a pair of

green Wellies. Around his neck hung a pair of glasses with spaghetti dangling from the rims.

"Why it's the older man from the Home Guards," thought Jake, "And the spaghetti on the glasses, just like The Bottom. I wonder if Brother Godric knows."

"I understand Brother Godric sent you," he barked. "I am Lord Baker, any friend of Brother Godric is a friend of mine. What's your name, lad?"

"It's Jake, Sir.!"

"Delighted to meet you, Jake," said Lord Baker, "and what is it that brings you to Severn Manor?"

"I can't tell you here," answered Jake. "Brother Godric just wants you to come with me and quickly!"

"Done," roared Lord Baker. "Bring my car around, James, and be lively. Do you drive, Jake?"

"No sir, I am not big enough to see over the wheel."

"Right, right," said Lord Baker, opening the door that Jake had entered moments before.

Jake followed Lord Baker to the driveway, where an old Rolls Royce stood waiting. The car was the same grey as Lord Baker's hair and it had a purple interior. Lord Baker opened the door for Jake and then slid in behind the wheel.

"We are off," he said enjoying the urgency of the

moment, but then stopping suddenly, he asked with a quizzical look, "Where are we going Jake?"

"To the abbey, the back way," said Jake.

"Right you are! Tally ho and we are gone," said Lord Baker.

The car moved slowly down the drive. It had a mind of its own and no intention of moving quickly. Finally, after much prodding from Lord Baker, it began to gain speed and move along quite smartly but then it decided to take a rest and stood fully still, no matter how much Lord Baker roared.

"We could have walked quicker," thought Jake.

After several irregular stops and starts they finally arrived at the back of the abbey. Jake led Lord Baker to the area of the old kitchen and called out to Sam and Brother Godric.

"Here we are," answered Brother Godric as he poked his head out of the secret door. "Hello to you, Lord Baker, I am so glad you could come and that you were at home."

"But what is this door? I didn't know it was here and I know a lot about this old abbey," replied Lord Baker.

"We didn't know it was here either," answered

Brother Godric. "More about that later. Now you must come and see what we have found. Come in, mind your head now; the door is small."

As Lord Baker entered the room he saw Sam and said, "So you have found this little girl. What a delight!"

"No," answered Sam, "I'm Jake's sister." She also noticed, with some alarm, the glasses with spaghetti hanging from them.

"Well, well ,well, well," stammered Lord Baker in his gruff voice, "I am delighted to meet you, my dear. Now Brother Godric, if it isn't the little girl that you have found, just what is it?"

"This!!" exclaimed Brother Godric pointing to the opened metal box.

"Oh my, my, my, my, my, amazing, amazing." Lord Baker examined the coins and said, "16th century for sure and in such good shape and the jewels, oh my, my, my. Where did they come from?"

With great enthusiasm, Brother Godric read Bede's letter.

"Good gracious, *The Legend of Pevensey Abbey* was true all along. There really was a leper Bede," Lord Baker said with awe. "I never thought in all the world that I would live to see this. Amazing, amazing, amazing! And to think, Brother Godric, that you and I have studied and explored this abbey together all these years and this treasure was right here all the time. How did you find it?"

"It was Fulham who led us to it," answered Sam. "He went down a tunnel and came back with a coin and a medal of St. Bede. They had probably fallen out when the lepers hid the box."

"The problem now is what shall we do with it?" said Brother Godric. "I don't think we should leave it here and I don't have enough protection for it in my workshop."

"Well, well, well," said Lord Baker. "Aren't you the lucky ones? You are doing just what our English law says to do if you find treasure. You must report your find to the government at once and since I am a constable that is me. And now the treasure becomes the property of the Crown, or the Queen or the country or whatever he mumbled. And you won't need to protect it."

"The Crown?" yelled Brother Godric, Sam and Jake. "The Crown? How can that be? We found it. Can't we even do what Bede said to do?" they asked, with utter disappointment..

"Now, now," said Lord Baker, realizing he had just dashed all their dreams. "Let me go on. When you report it at once, as you are doing, then you are entitled to the full amount of the market value of the treasure, which I can say with certainty, is a great deal, a great deal."

There was a moment of silence as Lord Baker's words sunk into the brains of the three finders and then suddenly and with great gusto they all sang out resounding hurrahs and hugged and kissed each other for a full five minutes. Fulham was totally confused by all this and kept running around in circles.

"I have a big safe at Severn Manor," added Lord Baker. "It will be as safe there as it would be in the Tower of London. Then I will call the British Museum and they can come out and take a look and tell us its value. Can you help me get it into the back of the car ?"

"Of course, of course," said Brother Godric, "but when we leave we must close up the tunnel and put the rocks that hid the secret door back in place."

"So there was a tunnel out as well as the hidden

door," observed Lord Baker. "Two definite protections, sounds like the Pharaohs of old. That is what they would have done. Wondrous!"

And so Lord Baker, Brother Godric, Jake, Sam and Fulham carried the metal box to Lord Baker's car and then they all went to Severn Manor and put it in the safe. Fulham loved the ride, he had never been in a car before. He sat between Jake and Sam and enjoyed the wind in his fur and smiled a ferret smile that was usually reserved only for other ferrets. When they all felt good about the safety of Bede's treasure, Lord Baker offered to take them back home. First they dropped Brother Godric at the workshop.

"We must all meet tomorrow," said Brother Godric, as he got out of the car. "We have a lot of things to talk about."

"Right you are," said Lord Baker. "I'll send James to pick you up at 3:30, by that time I will have talked to the British Museum."

"Fine," said Brother Godric, "tomorrow it is. Meet me after school, children, and we will go together."

Then Lord Baker headed his Rolls Royce toward Miss Bottomley's cottage at the edge of the village.

"Won't The Bottom be surprised to see us come

home in a Rolls Royce?" whispered Sam to Jake.

"I hope she is right outside to see it or she'll never believe us," said Jake.

As the grey Rolls pulled up to the cottage, The Bottom was indeed outside messing about in the pitiful garden. She turned around at the sound of the car and stood stock still as the children and Fulham stepped out.

Lord Baker sat at the wheel, very quietly, staring at The Bottom and then he slowly got out of the car, put on his glasses, spaghetti and all, and went up to The Bottom. Stammering, he said, "Could it be? Are you? My, my, my, my! Are you Alvira? Alvira in my Sunday school class? The girl with the beautiful smile, the smile of a goddess, of a nymph, of a fairy?"

Alvira Bottomley looked at Lord Baker and smiled a smile that came from deep inside her, the smile she had seen in the mirror that morning, truly a beautiful smile, a smile that made everyone else smile, Jake, Sam, Lord Baker and Fulham.

"Why yes, I am Alvira," she said. "Tell me who you are?"

"I am Edmund Baker, remember I sat next to you in Sunday school and was always transfixed by your smile."

"Oh my yes, yes now I remember," she answered. "Where have you been all these years? I have thought about you often. Excuse me, Edmund, you have a little spaghetti on your glasses. Let me help you."

"Why thank you Alvira, you have some too," said Lord Baker. "Let me help YOU."

Sam and Jake just stood and watched as Lord Baker and Alvira talked and talked as if they were the only people in the world, as if time were standing still for them. In fact Jake and Sam went inside and helped themselves to dinner, as much as they wanted. When they climbed the steps to bed, The Bottom and Lord Baker were still talking.

"I am not sure which is more amazing," said Jake to Sam as they lay in their beds that night in the little room at the top of the stairs, "Bede's treasure or The Bottom's smile."

"Maybe her smile is the real treasure of Pevensey Abbey," said Sam with a yawn.

Chapter 14

PLANS

The next morning The Bottom was singing *When You're Smiling* as she woke the children, and when they came down the steps she was twirling around the kitchen table and she had made pancakes for them and there were flowers on the table, and, wonder of wonder of wonders, The Bottom had combed her hair and put on a clean purple dress.

Her smile made the children smile, although they were a bit wary because, as you can imagine, they thought she might just be up to her old tricks.

"We must see Brother Godric and Lord Baker after school today," said Jake casually, so as not to arouse her curiosity.

"That's nice," she said, "but be home early because Edmund has asked us all to dinner at Severn Manor. I plan to wear purple because he likes purple too. He says he will pick us up in his machine. Isn't that lovely?"

"Yes, lovely," said Jake and Sam together backing out the door. They didn't know what to make of this new Bottom.

When they reported to Brother Godric the miracle that had taken place he just smiled and said, "Interesting!"

Lord Baker's chauffeur was waiting outside in the bright and shiny Rolls Royce when school was dismissed that afternoon. The other children watched as Jake, Sam, Brother Godric and Fulham of course, piled in, acting as if this happened everyday. They watched as the Rolls Royce went down the street and they watched as the Rolls Royce entered the tall gates of Severn Manor. They watched in silence and wondered and wondered.

When they arrived at the Manor, Lord Baker took them all to the drawing room where a large delicious tea had been laid and also a small one for Fulham.

"Now then! said Lord Baker as he bit into an enormous piece of cake and then spoke with his mouth full, "I have talked with Professor Flatman at the museum in London and he is convinced that Bede's box is worth at least one million pounds and the Crown will give you the full value. So what do you think of that, my friends?"

Jake, Sam and Brother Godric sat in stunned silence and could not move or speak.

"I had no idea it would be worth that much," said Brother Godric, "no, no idea. Amazing."

"Didn't Bede's letter say that the treasure should be used for the sick?" asked Jake.

"Yes," said Lord Baker "and it also stated that the finders should take some for themselves. I've discussed the problem with my solicitor and he feels that each of you is entitled to at least 100,000 pounds."

"Would that be enough to help me Mum and Dad?" asked Sam.

"Yes, yes," chortled Lord Baker, "and then some. Enough even for a pony or a motorbike or whatever it is that young children like today."

"I would really like to help Mum and Dad," Sam

said thoughtfully. " I would like to bring them here to live in Pevensey."

"Then that is what you shall do," said Lord Baker with an ever widening smile.

Jake looked at Brother Godric. "What will you do Brother Godric?" asked Jake.

"I've been thinking about that, Jake," said Brother Godric. "Perhaps I'll use a bit for more books and herbs and a bit of a sweet now and then."

"You'll still have a lot left after that," remarked Lord Baker.

"If Bede said the rest should be used for the sick," said Jake, as he reached for another biscuit, "maybe it should be used right here in the village that he ran to, right here in Pevensey. We don't even have a doctor here or a surgery or a clinic or a hospital. Maybe my Dad could help. He is a doctor you know."

Brother Godric's eyes began to sparkle. "Yes, yes, my boy, you are right. You are so right. Pevensey Abbey could return to what it was meant to be all along. Bede's treasure could help rebuild the abbey and open a clinic here. We could build it where the monk's hospital for lepers used to stand. There is plenty of room. It's perfect! It is what Bede would have wanted. Jake, you are a genius."

"It could be called *Bede's Clinic and Surgery,*" suggested Sam, "and Brother Godric, you could make all the medicines. You know enough about it."

"Oh. my dear," said Brother Godric, "I would have to go back to school for that and that is an expensive undertaking."

"You have the money now, my friend," Lord Baker reminded him.

"I do, don't I? Amazing!" said Brother Godric with a smile.

And so Lord Baker, Brother Godric, Jake and Sam talked right through their tea about all their exciting plans for the future and Fulham, full of lovely sweets, curled up in Jake's lap and listened to them all.

Chapter 15

THE DINNER

That evening Lord Baker did indeed gather The Bottom and Jake and Sam in his oh-so-brilliant car, and they, along with Brother Godric, went to Lord Baker's grand manor house for a celebration dinner. It was a most magnificent dinner served in a wondrous room: a red room it was, with great high ceilings filled with gold carvings. The chandeliers were crystal and sparkled with the light from the one hundred candles that were on the table and on the walls. Pure white china with a purple rim was on the table that was covered with a purple table cloth and there were purple crystal goblets too. As you can imagine, Lord Baker and The Bottom fit right in, what with Lord Baker's purple hair ribbons and purple shirt and tie and The Bottom's purple dress, shoes, and necklace.

The entire group had been looking forward to a good dinner for they knew that Lord Baker had a large farm and he would not have to depend on wartime ration tickets. They were not disappointed. When everyone was seated, Lord Baker asked Brother Godric to say a blessing and then he nodded to the head butler that dinner could begin. The servants then began a long parade of tray after tray after tray of lovely, glorious food: steaming soup, roast chickens with dumplings, sausages, prawns, turkey, oysters, crisp roast potatoes, sprouts, applesauce, home-made bread and butter, and for pudding, a lovely apple pie topped with fresh, smooth cream.

Jake and Sam enjoyed every spoonful and they also enjoyed watching The Bottom.

When Brother Godric was saying the blessing Miss Bottomley had trouble keeping her saliva in her mouth and when dinner finally appeared she had to hold on to the table so that she would not grab at the food before the servants had a chance to put it down.

She began to eat as they had seen her do at the cottage but then she would catch herself and try to appear to have manners. Lord Baker had a hard time keeping his eyes off of her; he was so charmed by her smile. And she kept smiling. But now it was truly a lovely smile; even Jake and Sam liked it, although they had a hard time accepting it.

During dinner everyone talked excitedly about finding the treasure and about their plans for *Bede's Clinic and Surgery*. They decided they could safely tell The Bottom now that everything had been taken care of by the British Museum. Then Lord Baker had another surprise.

"Alvira," he said to The Bottom. "what would you think of coming to live here at the manor, with the children of course? I have plenty of room and I noticed that your cottage is a bit shabby, well really shabby, no very, very shabby. Would you consider it? And then well, you know, if things worked out, perhaps one day, we could (he was blushing) well, perhaps we could marry. I have loved you for so long, ever since our school days."

Jake almost jumped up and screamed at Lord Baker, "You are making a big mistake! Don't do it!

Don't ever, ever do it. Never! Never!"

Brother Godric gave him a look that said, "Be quiet" and a hand that held him in his seat. He had watched many people change during his lifetime and he was seeing the first hints of change in The Bottom now.

"Why Edmund, really I am quite shocked by all this!" exclaimed The Bottom. "I need some time to think. Oh dear, perhaps another piece of pie will help."

A servant appeared with the pie and as Lord Baker looked on with a fond smile, Miss Bottomley devoured the pie in two bites.

"Yes, Edmund," she said, daintily wiping her mouth, "Yes, yes. Your plan is a good one. Jake, Sam and I will come here to live and Fulham, too, if that is all right."

"Why of course it's all right, my dear sweet Alvira with the beautiful smile," cooed Lord Baker.

"We won't stay for long," said Jake with relief. "Our parents will be able to come to Pevensey now and we will be with them," he said looking straight at The Bottom. "No more mean and nasty tricks," he said.

"No more fried Sam for dinner," said Sam out

loud.

"Now, now, Sam, you know that I was only teasing," said The Bottom as she watched for Lord Baker's reaction and kicked Jake under the table.

Lord Baker chose not to hear what Sam said. He was completely taken with Alvira and could not believe that she had a mean bone in her body. That however, would be something he would have to deal with in the future. At least, for now, Jake and Sam felt they had warned him.

And so it was that a clinic and surgery came to the village of Pevensey, that the Abbey of Our Lady of Pevensey was rebuilt, that Brother Godric became the village chemist and that Jake and Sam were reunited with their parents in the village where they had been evacuated. The Bottom did finally marry Lord Baker and she did change, although there were a quite a few times when she reverted to her old ways. Lord Baker would step in then and say, "Alvira darling, you really must not do that, you must not, you must NOT." And she would stop or mostly stop.

In June of 1940 Hitler's tanks rolled over France and the French came under his control; the danger to England and the children grew profoundly worse and the war continued for several more years. Jake and Sam did their part to help defeat Hitler, but those stories are for another day.

THE END
———————

8th June, 1946

To-day as we celebrate victory. I send this personal message to you and all other boys and girls at school. For you have shared in the hardships and dangers of a total war and you have shared no less in the triumph of the Allied Nations.

I know you will always feel proud to belong to a country which was capable of such supreme effort; proud, too, of parents and elder brothers and sisters, who by their courage and endurance and enterprise brought victory. May these qualities be yours as you grow up and join in the common effort to establish among the nations of the world unity and peace.

A message from King George the Sixth to the children.